OFF BOOK

NEUTRINOMAN AND LIGHTNINGIRL: A LOVE STORY,
EPISODE 4

ROBERT J. MCCARTER

LITTLE HUMMINGBIRD PUBLISHING

Off Book

Neutrinoman and Lightningirl: A Love Story, Episode 4

Copyright 2020 by Robert J. McCarter

Cover image: 123rf.com/profile_kitleong

Version 1.0, February 2020

ISBN: 978-1-941153-30-7

Find out more about this series at: Neutrinoman.com

Visit Robert's website at: RobertJMcCarter.com

Published by:

Little Hummingbird Publishing

P.O. Box 23518

Flagstaff, AZ 86002

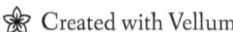 Created with Vellum

NEUTRINOMAN & LIGHTNINGIRL: A LOVE STORY

- Meteor Attack!
- Toxic Asset
- Protocol X
- Season 1 (Omnibus edition of Episodes 1 - 3)
- Off Book
- Hard Times (coming April, 2020)
- Elemental Factors (coming June, 2020)
- Season 2 (Omnibus edition of Episodes 4-6, coming August , 2020)

Find out the latest at Neutrinoman.com

1 / A QUIET MOMENT

WHAT HAPPENED AFTER BOY MET GIRL, AFTER THEY FOUND out they both had powers, after they saved the world together and shared a kiss? After they began defending the world against an alien aggressor and things got hard for both of them? After the girl pushed the boy away because of what was expected of them. After the girl broke up with the boy. After the girl saved the boy from those aliens and lost someone she cared about in the attack. After the boy bared his soul and told her that she was the personification of what he was fighting for, that she was what made the world worth defending, how she made him stronger not weaker. After she agreed to be his girlfriend and they agreed to be a mess together?

What happened after a hopefully happily ever after?

Have you ever wondered? After the initial romance, how does the couple stay together through tumultuous times? How do you save the world and stay in love, grow deeper in love?

If you were Nik Nichols aka Neutrinoman (that would be me) and Licia Lopez aka Lightningirl, that "being a mess together" meant holing up in a little A-frame cabin in Flagstaff, Arizona, that was nestled up against the ponderosa pine forest and playing Scrabble while a fire crackled in an old iron woodstove.

It was late, past midnight, and she was dressed in a fuzzy black bathrobe and I was in sweats, a blanket spread in front of the wood-stove and a game of Scrabble sitting between us, the tiles crawling all over the board in a game that was clearly near completion. It was dark outside and quiet, the red wine in our glasses from the local winery where we had our first date, a homemade ceramic platter with cheese and crackers on the blanket next to the Scrabble board, the taste of Munster and dry red wine lingering in my mouth. Her face was intent on the board as she chewed on her lower lip.

She was petite and alluringly feminine with dark, silky hair that was disheveled and cascading down past her shoulders, deep brown eyes, and a round face. She was beautiful and intelligent and powerful and I loved her, but I didn't really understand her. I wanted her, I needed her, but I didn't get her yet.

Yes, some of it was the whole differences between men and women, but we weren't just a man and a woman anymore. We were quantum-metamorphs, our powers bestowed upon us eighteen months ago when the cosmic rays struck and our accidents happened.

Me at the Palo Verde Nuclear Generating Station, she while working as a line woman for the local electric utility.

The woodstove had a glass front and the undulating yellow light was caressing her light brown skin, making her already beau-tiful face even more lovely. I couldn't get enough of that face, of those eyes, those lips. I wanted to caress her with the tenderness and intimacy of the firelight, but we had had our fill of that for the moment.

We'd been here for almost two weeks, after what happened at the Battle of Palo Verde where she saved my life but had to kill to do it. For the first time. After she quit the military's q-morph program. After she decided to stop being Lightningirl. After she agreed to be my girlfriend.

We used to be regular people with regular problems, but we were no longer quite human. We each can transform at a quantum level, her into a controlled electrical reaction in the form of a beautiful woman and me a controlled nuclear reaction in the form of a man.

We used to have simple lives and simple problems, and they were anything but now.

Powers changed things. Working for the military changed things. Taking lives changed things. Having our identities revealed changed things. Saving the world changed things.

I didn't understand her because of all of these things. And, if truth be told, I didn't understand myself. I liked to think that I was the same old Nik, the same guy who had cruised rather aimlessly through his twenties, who had gotten the job as a janitor at Palo Verde just so he could see the inside of a nuclear power plant, who did what he did during that accident, exposing himself to a lethal dose of radiation during the day the cosmic rays hit, because lives were at stake and it was the right thing to do.

But the powers and the saving the world and the falling in love all made it so much more complicated.

"Okay," Licia said, her eyes meeting mine, a grin on her face as she nodded down at her tiles. After all that saving the world, we both need a whole lot of mundane, and this late Scrabble game was just about perfect for that.

I shifted away from the crackling fire a bit, my left side quite baked from its lovely radiant heat, the distant scent of smoke in the air.

Licia picked up four tiles, her smile growing wider. "Double letter on the 'O,' triple word, that's thirty-three points!"

She added "OXIC" to the "T" in "TOAST," forming "TOX-IC." She looked at me, but now her smile was rather shy. Was this an opening? A conversation she wanted to have? Tom Tyree aka Toxicwasteman was something of a frenemy. He was a villain, there was no doubt about that, but he wanted to defeat the aliens too and had taken an interest in me.

One that wasn't always comfortable for me and was never comfortable for Licia.

"Nice one," I said with a nod. "You've been holding onto that X for a long time."

She nodded, her lips pursed. "I was waiting for the right word."

"I don't trust him, you know," I said, easing into the opening.

"Completely," she said, taking a sip of wine.

"What?" I asked.

"You don't trust him... completely," she said, her eyebrow arched and gaze appraising.

And there it was. Since I had met Tom, my trust for the military had decreased as I interacted with him. It didn't feel good, but she had a point.

"I don't trust him," I said, "except when it comes to defeating the aliens."

She took a deep breath. "Even though he will lie, he will cheat, he will do whatever it takes to—"

"Defeat the aliens," I finished, interrupting her.

She pursed her lips and nodded. "He is not like you, Nik. Just because you both have the same goal, don't fool yourself. He is using you, and when he's done with you..." she ended in a shrug, her robe opening just a bit, but I kept my eyes locked with hers—this was not the time to get distracted.

I sighed. "I know. It's..." I leaned forward across the board, close enough so that I could smell the wine and cheese on her breath, my voice a whisper. "I think I trust the military less. What would they have done with Sarah, the alien I saved? Interrogated her? And how? What kinds of measures would they have resorted to? She is so much like us I think there has to be a way to stop all this. And what hasn't the military told us? You know that there is a lot. Colonel Williams is a great guy, I'd follow him just about anywhere, but he has to follow orders. I don't trust General Markus any farther than I can throw him. I..."

I stopped when I realized that my face was flushed and my tone had gotten loud. Too loud. I leaned back and nodded. "I don't trust him and I don't trust the military." I gave her my best smile and added, "But I do trust you."

She smiled back, it was sweet, but brief, a small reward, but not what she was after. "And..." she prompted, giving me no direction on which way she was thinking the conversation should go.

I took a sip of wine to give myself time to think, letting the rich, velvety flavor linger.

My shoulders fell. "And... it's too much. It's too damn much. Just because I can fly, because I can shoot neutrino bolts, because I can explode, they both want... they all want..."

I was breathing too fast and felt tears stinging my eyes. I wanted Licia to know all of me but thought it might be too soon for this, but she had agreed to be a mess with me.

"There is an alien threat," I continued, "one strong enough to point an asteroid at us, one clever enough to almost maneuver me into setting off the super volcano below Yellowstone. I'm just a regular guy and barely know how to use these powers, how the hell am I supposed to save the world? Why does everyone want me to save the world?"

I trailed off and looked back at Licia. There was compassion written on her beautiful face. She licked her lips and nodded. "Nik," she said slowly. "Why do *you* think *you* should save the world?"

I was too hot. I wanted to run out into the freezing cold mountain night. It was so quiet, just the crackling of the fire while Licia stared at me. This here, this was intimacy, true intimacy, way beyond the physical. I still worried that if she really knew me that she wouldn't want me. But I couldn't hide this from everyone, and she was one of the only people on the planet that could understand.

"Because..." I began, taking a deep breath. "I do have this power. I have to try."

She nodded and reached out and I let her take my hand. She kissed it gently. "You are a good man, Nik. This, more than anything, gives me hope."

I blinked, the tears so close to escaping. Hope for our world? Hope for our relationship? What did that give her hope for?

I opened my mouth to speak when my phone chimed, and at the same time, Licia's landline rang. Her brow furrowed, but she held my gaze for a breath before getting up.

"Hello," she said. "Yes, Colonel Williams. What's going on?"

I flipped my phone open and read the text. It was from Williams:

Report to Palo Verde at 0800. Urgent meeting. Bring Ms. Lopez.

Licia came back, her arms wrapped around her chest as if she was cold in that big fluffy robe. "We have to get up early. Let's get some sleep. We'll have more time."

I nodded and smiled. I got up and pulled her into a hug.

I didn't know it, but everything was about to change, and it would be a long time before we'd have a chance to talk like this again.

2 / SARAH SPEAKS

THE VIDEO WAS GRAINY, BUT CLEAR ENOUGH. IT SHOWED A picture of the alien Sarah dressed in a silver jumpsuit, like when I had rescued her from her crashed spaceship. The classic *The Day the Earth Stood Still* look. She looked good, the cut on her forehead was healing well, her long blond hair was pulled back, her blue eyes intense, her youthful Nordic looks making it hard to believe that she was not from this planet. The audio was crisp and clear.

This video had been received by mail, sent to Diane Madison at WNN on a thumb drive. The world hadn't seen it yet, but Diane was going to air it this evening.

Licia, Colonel Williams, General Markus, Jennifer Johnson, and I were in a hushed little conference room at the Palo Verde Nuclear Generating Station, the lights off, the glow of the large screen making everyone look a little bit ghostly.

I was tired. After our late-night Scrabble session and our conversation, I hadn't slept much. We'd gotten up early and hit the road before 6:00 a.m. neither of us talking much on the way down from Flagstaff. I think we both had too much on our minds. We didn't know what we were being called in for and Licia was only here as a favor to Williams. She didn't want to be anywhere near the military's q-morph program.

"I am known as Sarah," the tall alien began on the video. She looked nervous. Behind her was a flat white wall, no clues whatsoever to her location. "I represent the Arcturian Alliance. I am no one, but I will speak for you and all will listen. This is our way."

The room was dead quiet, all eyes fixed on the screen. Sarah's smooth forehead was furrowed and she spoke slowly as if the words were hard to say, her accent strange and unidentifiable.

"Your planet has been classified as threat. We have been listening and watching you for sixty Earth years. We have been studying you. You are an immature and violent species. The Arcturian Alliance has determined that extermination is required. Several attempts have been made and have failed."

The meteor attack that started all this madness and the "Incident at Yellowstone" came leaping to mind. I wondered if there were others.

"None then spoke on your behalf," she continued. "I speak now."

General Markus caught my eye and gave me a small nod, his round face relaxing a bit and his green eyes sharp. Releasing her had been my idea, and it had caused a major fight between me and the general. This video was starting to sound like Sarah was keeping her end of the bargain. That we did the right thing.

"I have been to your planet. I have witnessed the kindness and compassion of the yellow one. When we fought, he saved me. I am no one but he saved me, he saved others, he fought for my release from your military. So now I speak on your behalf and hostilities will stop.

"While I speak, while the council listens and debates, there will be no more attacks by the Arcturian Alliance. This is our way."

She stopped, her head falling and her blue eyes hidden. I could see her chest rise and then fall in a shuddering exhale. When she finally looked back at the camera, the wrinkles on her forehead were gone and her blue eyes were hard. It looked to me like she was about to go off script.

"Look in your hearts, people of Earth. Find compassion for one another. Stop your wars and fighting. Stop putting the needs of the individual over the whole. Stop killing each other. This is your chance to change, your one chance. Once I speak, once they listen, the decision will be final. We will either leave you be or we will destroy you for the sake of all."

I sat there blinking, my chest tight. I couldn't breathe and it didn't sound like anyone else was breathing.

"Look to the yellow one," she said. "Be more like him. I am called Sarah. I am no one, but because of the yellow one, I speak for you."

The video ended and Jennifer turned on the lights. The room was silent, the air thick and heavy, all eyes on me. Colonel Williams rubbed his salt-and-pepper hair and shook his head. General Markus had this faraway look on his round face. Jennifer just stood there in her ever-present white lab coat, her arms wrapped around herself just like she was cold.

I am Neutrinoman, the "yellow one," and what Sarah just said made my heart pound hard in my chest and sweat trickle down my back. She was asking the world to be more like me. She was holding me up as an example. It's what Licia and I just talked about. It was too much. I wanted to bolt, to run away. To leave all this behind and just have a normal life with Licia. I didn't want to be the hero.

Under the table, Licia grabbed my hand and squeezed it hard. Her soft brown eyes in her beautiful face were compassionate as she looked at me.

She didn't speak, her lips pressed into a thin line. She knew what this fight with the Arcturian Alliance had cost her, had cost me. She knew how things were getting more complicated. She had been with me when I had been served last week. Some people of

Las Vegas suing me because of the damage the alien's meteor attack had done there, citing my incompetence in not completely destroying the threat.

Peace had come, but for how long? And if Diane Madison outing me as Neutrinoman wasn't enough, if this new lawsuit wasn't enough, I now had an alien telling the entire world to stop fighting and to look to me as an example.

It was just too damn much.

3 / WHAT HAPPENS IN VEGAS...

I HAVE COME TO KNOW AND UNDERSTAND THE BEAUTY OF THE desert. It's not a flashy beauty like the tropics, it's a quiet beauty, deep and abiding, entirely mysterious.

Quinn Rask, my new dark-haired and muscular q-morph partner, drove my 1990 Ford Focus down US-93 in the northwestern corner of Arizona between Kingman and Las Vegas. It's a long, lonely stretch of desert with plentiful cactus and craggy hills in the distance.

Spring had come and with it hope. After Sarah's video, the full truth of the alien attacks on our planet had come to light. The governments of the world had even started releasing details they had about previous alien visits: Roswell, New Mexico in 1947 (it wasn't a weather balloon); the Rendlesham Forest incident in 1980 (alien ships did land in England); Japan Air Lines flight 1628 in 1986 (alien ships seen over Alaska); the Phoenix Lights in 1997 (not airplanes); and more.

I had done more interviews and had become a celebrity. I was dealing with paparazzi when I was out in the world and then with endless training when I was with the military.

Some lawyers had taken up defending me against the Las Vegas lawsuit pro bono, wanting to grab a piece of the limelight, which I was happy to share. Still, it took too much of my time.

This "speaking" Sarah was doing was of an unknown length with a decision-making process we couldn't fathom. Everyone was worried the attacks would resume. Just because Sarah implored us to "stop killing each other" and had promised that "we will destroy you for the sake of all" if they perceived the need, didn't mean we could change.

The US was still at war in Iraq and Afghanistan, the Middle East was a disaster, and fighting terrorism was a major pastime here since 9/11. School shootings. Gun violence. Murder a daily occurrence in all big cities. There was no shortage of humans killing humans.

The threat of annihilation often made us less logical, not more.

And the worst part was that I hadn't had much time with Licia. Not the kind of time we needed, not the kind of conversation we were about to have over that Scrabble game in front of the crackling woodstove.

I stared out of the car at the dirt and sage brush whipping by me. The signs of spring were not overt in the desert, but they were there. Growing green grasses, instead of the usual brown, the lighter green of new growth on the sage brush.

"Are you going to be this pensive the whole trip?" Quinn asked, his blue eyes boring into me as we roared down the two-lane road at ninety miles per hour, the fastest my little Ford could manage.

I looked at him and smiled, but it didn't work very well. I only managed a grimace. As much as I liked Quinn, I finally had some R&R and was spending it with him instead of Licia on our crazy "off book" mission. The military thought we were going to Las Vegas to blow off some steam. In truth we were going there in search of Chaosboy. Since our "little heist" on the train I couldn't stop thinking about him, about how he could bend probabilities with his will, about how he left a wake of chaos and bad luck for others, about how blasé he was about collateral damage.

An alien threat. Overwhelming celebrity. A lawsuit. Not enough time with Licia. Chaosboy and the damage he could cause. I had reason to be pensive.

"Because if you going to be big wet blanket, then I think we should turn around now," he said. Quinn had this odd accent that is impossible to place. He said it's because of his Army brat upbringing, spending the first sixteen years of his life in five different countries in Europe, and his French mother.

I took a deep breath and tried to shake it off. Quinn was still staring at me as we roared down the road. It made me nervous, but I understood that it wasn't dangerous for him. Quinn is a q-morph—quantum metamorph—like Licia and I. But unlike us, his powers are always present, just like Chaosboy and Byte. And that makes him sound like a quantum biomorph, but he earns the "meta" with what he can do.

During the day the cosmic rays hit, he was working in the Relativistic Heavy Ion Collider in Upton, New York. He was inside the collider inspecting some of the sensors when the collider was accidentally triggered. The collider is a 3.8-kilometer track where ions traveling at relativistic speed (a significant portion of the speed of light) collide so physicists can study the primordial form of matter that existed shortly after the Big Bang. Those particles went through Quinn's body and mixed with those cosmic rays turning him into the q-morph he is today.

He doesn't have a single superhero name like most of us do. Actually, he has a lot of superhero names, but no one knows that they all belong to him: The Hammer, Stretchman, Jumper, and others. Actually, he's the reason that most counts of the q-morphs created that day in 2003 are too high. He can control his body at a molecular level and, in reality, is each of those q-morphs.

And this is why I didn't need to be worried about him looking at me while he was driving down a two-lane highway like a maniac. In his normal form, a handsome and muscular 6'4", he has the best reflexes on the planet and amazing peripheral vision. He could look at me and still drive safely.

But this isn't his natural form. I think it's the body he wanted to have when he was young. He was in his late fifties when the accident happened, but he looks like he's about thirty now.

"Come on, Nik," he said. "We need to have some fun. We've been cooped up for weeks."

"We're going to Vegas for a reason," I said.

"Yes! To gamble and drink and chase women—"

"To find Chaosboy," I said, interrupting. "To stop him."

Quinn was silent, his eyes turning to the road, the smile melting off his face. He ran his right hand through his jet-black hair in a gesture I have come to understand signals nervousness for him. His hair was slicked back and perfect as always. The gesture was completely unnecessary.

"How do you know he is there?" Quinn asked quietly.

I sighed. We had been over this. "Chaosboy has a fan club, a private group on Yahoo. I'm a member."

"And how did you get into the group?"

"Byte got me in last month." Byte was Tom Tyree's (aka Toxicwasteman's) tech guru. She was a q-morph that could control the Internet with her mind and is part of LoVE (League of Villains Extraordinaire).

"Chaosboy and Byte are both part of LoVE," he said slowly. "Why would she do this thing?"

I shrugged, but I suspected why. There was something Tom and his gang wanted me to do. I knew that Byte had probably run one of her computer simulations, known that evidence of Chaosboy being close might draw me out. I knew that they were probably manipulating me, but that didn't change the fact that I wanted to have a serious conversation with him. That I wanted to bring him in.

The time I spent with LoVE changed me. I no longer doubted that we both had the same goal (eliminate the alien threat, save the world) but it was their methods that disturbed me. I had also come to believe that LoVE was approaching the problem in ways far more innovative than the military.

So maybe this was some convoluted way to get me to do something, but it was in alignment with something I wanted to do. So be it.

"And what will we do with this Chaosboy if we catch him?" Quinn asked.

I stared back out at the desert again, trying to catch more signs of spring, the light green of new growth, the color of a blooming cactus.

In truth, I didn't know. I wanted Chaosboy stopped, but how far would I be willing to go to do that?

LICIA DIDN'T KNOW WHAT WE WERE UP TO. SHE THOUGHT WE were just out for some fun, some male bonding, cutting loose time. And oddly, she wasn't hurt that I was spending time off without her. Well, that wasn't odd for her, but odd for other women I have known.

She had been rather withdrawn since she left the program ten weeks ago. At first, she tried to go back to her job at Arizona Public Service (APS), but since the world knew who she was and what she looked like, crowds would gather when she was doing dangerous work on high-tension power lines.

She had a fan club, and members of it would roam Northern Arizona and tell others of her location if they found her.

Lately, Licia had been holed up in her cabin backing the forest south of Flagstaff. Taking long walks, wearing a blonde wig and dark glasses so her neighbors didn't recognize her, trying to have something of a normal life. But there was no "normal" for us anymore.

"You thinking of her?" Quinn asked. He was still driving my old Focus and we were past the Hoover Dam and Lake Mead and were headed down towards Boulder City and then Vegas. From here we could see the sprawl of Las Vegas laid out over the flat desert below.

"Yeah," I said.

"I could help if you like, I could—" he said, and I knew what was coming.

"No... please, Quinn. That would just make it..." I trailed off because it was too late. Quinn was morphing, the strange sound of it emanating from his side of the car. It's a disturbingly organic sound: kind of like a cross between flowing water and crickets chirping. His jet-black hair suddenly started growing long, his features changing, his limbs thinning and his body growing shorter. From the bulky 6'4" frame of Quinn Rask to the lithe body of Licia Lopez. Or at least a close enough reproduction to be completely unnerving.

He got the body proportions right, his new body dressed in shorts and black tank top, but the face wasn't quite there. The cheekbones were too high, the eyes a bit too big, the lips puffy. And his blue eyes were still there instead of Licia's brown. When Quinn changed, for some reason his eyes didn't.

"Hey, big boy," Quinn-Licia said. "Don't be sad little puppy dog. I am right here." The voice was feminine but definitely not Licia. It takes Quinn a long time to get good at another form. It takes a lot of practice. He wasn't that good at Licia.

"Stop it."

"But hey," she-he said as she-he looked down at her-his chest, "I've always thought these were a bit inadequate."

The clicky/squishy sound resumed and Quinn-Licia went from a B-cup to a D-cup, her breasts swelling under the black tank top. "That better? You like?"

I looked away. That weird face, that strange voice, it was just too much. I stared at this abandoned western-themed casino, built to look like an old fort, as we passed it. I didn't want that nightmare version of Licia to stick with me. And for the record, I have never found anything about her physicality to be inadequate.

Quinn's transformation sound started up again for a minute or so. "It's okay now," he said in his normal, deep voice. "Sorry, thought you might find that funny."

"Don't *ever* do that again," I said, glad to see him back.

He smiled at me, this perfect white-toothed grin. "Of course not."

We drove in silence the rest of the way to the Golden Nugget Casino on Freemont Street in old Las Vegas. We knew Chaosboy was there. We had a plan.

INTERLUDE 1: QUINN

"Quinn Rask," Licia said, her jaw set, her arms folded across her chest, her normally soft brown eyes hard and dangerous. It was midday and we were working on the new greenhouse at Casita de Soledad, our isolated home in central Arizona where Homeland Security basically kept us under house arrest.

After the madness was all over and we signed the Quantum Metamorph Accord in 2020, this is where we ended up. My love and I in the high desert of Arizona building our own home to keep ourselves busy and me busily doing a lot of navel gazing writing these memoirs.

Licia's electrical powers made her very good with plants and this was the second greenhouse we had taken on. The foundation and flagstone floor were laid and we were now getting ready to put up some posts to support the roof.

I had just shorts and work boots on, my skin pasty white as always—it dealt with the UV light in a different way. Licia had a black tank top on, her already brown skin slightly darker from all the time we had been spending outside. Her silky black hair was pulled back into a ponytail.

It has been over twenty years since all of this began, since the cosmic rays hit and we got our powers, but Licia still looks to be in her thirties and so do I. Our frequent transformations into our quantum metamorph selves seem to be keeping us young, slowing the aging process, which means we might be stuck out here alone in the desert for another fifty years or more. So the building was partially about keeping us busy, but also about making our time out here more enjoyable because it seemed we were going to have a lot of it.

I spent about a month away from writing as I dug the foundation, mixed cement, and laid in the floor. But it was eating at me. This story has kind of taken on a life of its own now, the story has to be told. I've started a new schedule. I get up early and write for an hour or two before we start on the greenhouse.

Licia knows I need it and has been supportive. When I came out today, she was already here and working and asked me what I was writing about. I told her Quinn had just been introduced.

"So you're finally to it," she said, shaking her head.

I shrugged. Back when I was first starting this project, she asked me if I was writing it because of "him." And in truth that was one part of it, and Quinn is that "him." We'll get to it all, but for now let me say that our relationship was more than a little complicated.

"I hope this helps you," she said. What she didn't add, and I think she meant was, "because this isn't going to help me."

Quinn's relationship with Licia, and really all of us, was... I wish I had a different word, one that better described the breadth and depth of it all, but "complicated" is all I can come up with. It wasn't at first, but boy did it get complicated. There is a residue left there that I would love to shed myself of. I don't know if writing about him will make it better or worse. I guess there is only one way to find out.

4 / NABBING CHAOSBOY

IN THE CAR SITTING IN THE PARKING GARAGE OF THE GOLDEN Nugget, Quinn started transforming again. That sound always sent a chill down my spine. What he did just wasn't natural. I looked away. I didn't want to witness it.

"It's a little hurtful, you know," he said, his voice feminine and sultry.

"What?" I asked, looking at him. He was now a statuesque blond dressed in heels and a tight red cocktail dress. This was one of his go-to forms he had practiced and was good at. He called her Sadie, so I'll refer to Quinn as this when he is her. (His transformations can certainly challenge the use of pronouns.)

"You are disgusted by who I am," Sadie said, a pouty frown on her face.

I took a deep breath. I couldn't believe he was bringing this up now. Here.

"We are partners now," she said. "We need to embrace each other's unique capabilities." She then pulled up the front of her strapless dress, in a move that is entirely distracting to the hetero-sexual male. Sadie was well endowed so it was quite the show.

As I tried to come up with something to say I realized that when Quinn turned into Licia earlier and then into Sadie, he didn't leave any clothing behind. His clothing as Quinn had been part of his form. Part of him.

"You've been naked this whole time?" I asked. "Seriously, dude? That is not cool."

Sadie shrugged, her blue eyes looking me up and down. The eyes were the one part of Quinn that was still part of Sadie and the lecherous look she gave me freaked me out. "Clothing just gets in the way, don't you think?"

I got out of the car and slammed the door. "Oh, hell, Quinn. What is wrong with you?"

Sadie got out of the car, her movements slow and sensuous. "Do you know how much fun I can have with this body in a town like this?" Her feminine hands raked up and down her hourglass figure, the dress leaving little (or just enough) to the imagination.

I sighed. "Just stick to the plan, okay?"

She shrugged and tugged her dress up again. "Chaosboy won't be able to resist me."

Of that, there could be no doubt.

———

My intel put Chaosboy playing craps in the Golden Nugget right now. He was having what he called one of his "Chaos Meets" with a few of his fans. It was basically him showing off to a crowd and raking in lots of money from the casino. His groupies bet with him and made money too.

There were reports of previous versions of this on his Yahoo group. Since they're such a public thing he really had to bend prob-ability hard for the casino to not catch on too soon. Inevitably someone got hurt. A stumble leading to a broken arm in Reno, a fatal heart attack outside of Phoenix, and lots of dropped electronics.

The weird thing was, his groupies didn't seem to mind. They seemed to get off on the danger of being near him. This world has no shortage of weirdos.

Our plan was simple. Quinn—or rather Sadie—would go in playing the role of a groupie and lure him away up to her room. Not that we had a room, he was to get Chaosboy to the elevators where I would be waiting.

I had a Bluetooth headset on and was listening through Sadie's phone. She had dialed me once she had spotted him and then stashed the phone (I didn't know where and didn't want to know). The Golden Nugget is a bit of a labyrinth, just like all casinos, and I was hanging out in the south tower lobby at the end of a long hallway with garish orangish and brown carpet that I tried not to look too much at. The hall went past the outdoor swimming pool, large windows showing the oval pool and waterfall (this is before the shark tank with a slide through it went in).

"Hey, Red," Sadie said through the phone line. And I do have to admit that she has a wicked sultry voice, a bit Demi Moore, a bit Scarlett Johansson.

"Well, hello there, beautiful," Chaosboy said with his Irish accent. "You're just in time to blow on my dice for luck."

"On this peach of a day," Sadie said. "I'd love to." The phrase "peach of a day" was the code phrase from the Yahoo group. It identified Sadie as one of his core groupies. There was then a very exaggerated blowing sound and a boyish giggle from Chaosboy. I can imagine how Sadie bent over giving him a fine view of her epic cleavage.

No. I don't want to imagine that.

There was a lot of background noise, his cheering groupies, overlapping conversation, the jangle of slot machines, but I could hear pretty well. I went over to the small Starbucks near the elevators and got a coffee. I was nervous, and knew the caffeine probably wouldn't help, but I needed something to divert my attention from Sadie seducing Chaosboy.

Not that it was much of a seduction. I suspect Chaosboy was pretty sure he'd get "lucky" at all of these. He probably didn't even need to bend probability to do it.

I pulled the Red Sox baseball cap low on my head and adjusted my mirror shades. This amounted to my disguise. It wasn't much, but enough. No one recognized me.

There were a few small tables in front of the Starbucks and I took a seat and waited. I listened over the phone to the cheering as Chaosboy had an improbable run at the craps table, as Sadie gushed at his brilliance as Chaosboy did his occasional boyish giggle.

The coffee was bitter and I drank it slowly. By the time I was down to the cold dregs, the "Chaos Meet" was breaking up and Sadie had convinced Chaosboy to go to her room.

———

HE WAS TWENTY-ONE, SHORT, WITH FLAMING RED HAIR AND green eyes. He was wearing white pants and shirt and a straw hat, the kind of outfit some Florida mobster might wear. Sadie towered over him in her heels. Chaosboy had the biggest damn grin on his face as they walked past the Starbucks to the bank of elevators.

I relaxed a little. It didn't look like he suspected, and he didn't even glance my way when they passed. He was telling her a dirty joke about an Irish priest and a donkey, one I will do you the favor of not repeating.

After they passed, I tossed my coffee cup in the trash and ambled towards the elevator. Sadie made a show of bending over to press the up button and Chaosboy took the opening and stared at her ass. I shook my head, the two of them were just a pair. Sadie really looked like the right kind of dumb blond that would go for Chaosboy.

The elevator door dinged, some tourists spilled out before some more got in. Chaosboy made a step towards it but Sadie held him back. "Maybe we can get lucky, Red," she said. "Maybe we can get an elevator to ourselves."

Chaosboy looked her up and down (his head came up to her bosom, so it's more looking up than down) and grinned. It wasn't long until an empty elevator opened up and they walked in.

I walked in right behind them. Well, I almost didn't. I was positioned properly, only a few steps away, but somehow a guest with a huge trolley of luggage got in between me and the elevator at the last moment. Very unlucky.

Quite ungracefully, I plow right through the middle, spilling their luggage on the floor, and stumbled into the elevator just as it closed.

"Hey, lad," Chaosboy said. "This here is a private party."

"Yes, it is," I said, grabbing him by the lapels of his fancy white suit and slamming him against the back of the elevator.

He hit with an "oomph" and then the elevator suddenly stopped as Sadie hit the red emergency stop button. Sadie didn't turn back into Quinn. It was part of the plan, if we could confuse Chaosboy in any way during this it was worth a shot.

I kept him pinned to the back of the elevator with one hand and took off my sunglasses.

"Neutrino!" Chaosboy said. "What is this?"

"It's time for us to have a long talk. A very long talk."

———

WITH A LITTLE HELP FROM CHAOSBOY, THAT REQUIRED A little coercion from me, we managed to make it to the roof of the Golden Nugget's Carson Tower without interruption. It's a flat expanse of dull white with a waist-high wall all around. We were twenty-two stories up in the air and I didn't think it would be easy for Chaosboy to escape us.

Except once we got up there, once the door slammed behind us, once I let go of his neck, his demeanor changed. Radically.

"Well, Neutrino, I'm mighty glad you got my meetin' invite," he said as he strolled across the roof like he was taking a walk on the beach. There was a swagger to his step and a lilt in his voice that made me want to punch him.

"And Quinn," he said, turning to Sadie. "As much as I enjoy ya like this, ya can drop the disguise. We know all about ya, lad."

Sadie looked at me and I nodded. The click-squish sound emanated from him again and soon he was back to Quinn.

It was hot up here, over a hundred degrees, and I was starting to sweat. "What is this?" Quinn asked, looking at me.

"Chaosboy, here," I said, gesturing to the still strutting redhead, "and his gang set this all up. He was expecting us."

"You knew?" Quinn asked.

"I suspected, but it doesn't matter. We can still do what we came here to do."

"Okay, gents," Chaosboy said. "If we're done with pleasantries, let's get down to it." He trotted over to the north edge of the roof that bordered the outdoor ground-level pool and courtyard below and hopped up on the low wall, a big grin on his face.

Quinn rushed over and said, "Don't jump."

I took my time. I wasn't worried about Chaosboy hurting himself. Quinn didn't have much firsthand experience with him yet. Chaosboy was in no danger. I was beginning to doubt that we would be able to contain him, though. I was casting about for a plan when he started talking.

"Your mission, gentlemen," he began in a comical attempt at a deep voice, "should ya decide to accept it, is to stop the q-morph known as Gaia from causing major loss of life in the Las Vegas area and to, if you're able, bring said q-morph onto our side in the battle against the Arcturian Alliance."

He stopped, his hands spread wide, a huge grin on his face. Quinn and I were about five feet away.

Chaosboy pulled a keycard out of his pocket and tossed it to me. "That is for the penthouse suite. Ya have it for the night. A dossier on Gaia is in there—it won't self-destruct or anythin', so don't ya worry. The odds are long on this one, lads," he said, looking at me. "So ya will need your little firefly if you have any chance of capturing Gaia alive." By "little firefly" he was referring to Lightningirl. As I stood there, I hoped to be around when he called her that in person. "There is a plane waitin' for her in Flagstaff. Details in the suite."

Quinn and I stood there with our mouths open. In truth I had suspected this as a setup, but not to this degree. A mission? And from the *Mission Impossible* speech it sounded like a hard one. And who the hell was Gaia?

His smile broadened and he looked to Quinn. "If Sadie ever really wants a good time... Well, I'm game."

He took a step back on the wall and looked down before meeting our gazes again and continued in his not-so-deep voice. "As always, should anyone get caught or killed in this mission, LoVE, the League of Villains Extraordinaire, will disavow any knowledge of your actions."

He got this blank look on his face and then stepped off the wall, falling out of sight.

5 / MISSION IMPROBABLE

CHAOSBOY SURVIVED. OF COURSE HE DID. BUT YOU WOULDN'T believe me if I told you how. Or maybe you would. You've heard the stories of him, and these things for most q-morphs are really exaggerated. For him, not so much.

In some ways I suspected this was easy for him because of where we were. Chaosboy was created by the accident on Freemont Street. The Golden Nugget is on Freemont Street.

We were atop the south tower and that didn't face Freemont Street, but let's just say we were in the epicenter of his "luck."

The towers of the Golden Nugget surround the pool area. After he jumped, Quinn and I rushed over and saw what happened.

The little guy was falling with a grin on his face looking at us and waving enthusiastically with one hand while holding onto his hat with the other. He was headed for the roof over the conference center that fans out below the tower and borders the pool area. Then, out of nowhere a huge breeze rushed through the courtyard, shoving Chaosboy over the roof, over the sunbathing tourists and into the pool. It was a freak wind out of nowhere, a million—no more like a billion—to one. A big splash and then moments later he was out of the pool and walking calmly away.

Seconds later, I heard the crunch of steel and honking horns over on Casino Center Boulevard. The chaos left behind in the wake of his lucky fall.

"We should—" Quinn began.

"Don't bother," I said. "We lost him as soon as I let go of his scrawny neck."

Quinn gave me a look but didn't question further. We went down to the suite to find out about this "Mission Impossible."

⸺

THE SUITE WAS MAGNIFICENT. TWO LARGE BEDROOMS, A common area with a bar adjoining the two, and floor-to-ceiling windows overlooking old Las Vegas. More awful orange and brown carpet, but up here, with this view, I could live with it.

Next to the brown couch was a thick manila folder and a laptop sitting open, the screen said, "Press Enter."

We sat down on the couch and I tapped the enter key. A video came up of Tom Tyree. He's got his usual wolfish grin on his face. The background was of a nice room done in shades of brown. Looking around I can tell that he was filmed right here in this suite.

"Don't bother, Neutrino," he said. "We did film this here, but we are long gone."

It's frankly eerie how close Byte, the q-morph that is one with the internet, and her simulations are. And scary.

"And welcome, Quinn," he continued. "I look forward to us meeting in person one of these days. You are a fine addition to our mutual battle against the Arcturian Alliance. I believe you will soon come to know, as our friend Neutrino here has, that it will take all of us working together to defeat them."

Quinn looked at me, his brow furrowed. I just shrugged my shoulders and nodded.

"But for today, we've got a crisis brewing. Gaia is a powerful q-morph that has recently surfaced." The laptop showed a picture of a dark-skinned African woman dressed in a kaftan that flowed loosely around her body. Her brown eyes were intense, as was the grim frown was on her face. She was standing outside in front of a devastated area. It looked like it was recently a forest, but there was not much left but ragged stumps and browning foliage.

"Her name is Jena Grange. She was born in England but spent much of her life as an ecological activist in Africa. Here she is standing in front of a recently destroyed rainforest in the Democratic Republic of the Congo that was cut down to make room for cattle grazing."

The picture changed to show a large hole in the ground, edged with crumbling asphalt, a house slumping into it. "She became Gaia when this sinkhole swallowed her on that day in 2003 when the Earth was bathed in the cosmic rays that changed us all. Jena was presumed dead, but recent events have made us believe that she survived. That she is bent on the destruction of the human race. That she is in the United States now and her target is Las Vegas."

On the screen Tom blinked and rubbed at his long chin, his face becoming grim. "This is a distraction we cannot afford. We don't know her target yet, but we expect to know in the next twelve hours."

Tom paused, looking slightly to the left and then to the right like he was looking Quinn and me over. "I know you have some question, so I will answer them. But believe me when I tell you that time is of the essence."

He then looked to the right, at me. "Neutrino, you must get Lightningirl here and you must not contact the military. You need Lightningirl to have a chance in hell of catching Gaia, and if the military gets involved the loss of life goes up. Way up.

"I know this puts you in an awkward spot with your masters. But please trust me here. This is the only way."

He then turned to the left, looking right at Quinn. "Don't try to take Gaia on directly. She is too powerful. Follow Neutrino's lead."

Tom took a deep breath, clasping his hands in front of him.

"The rest that we know," Tom continued on the screen, "including details of Byte's simulations, are in the folder. Good luck." The wolfish grin returned to Tom's face. "This message, will in fact, self-destruct in five seconds."

LICIA CAN BE TOUGH TO TALK TO ON THE PHONE. HER emotional cues are not always verbal... often they are not. They are mostly visual and mostly subtle. A raising of one eyebrow, a brief frown, a quick roll of the eyes.

I knew that when I dialed her from one of the suite's bedrooms looking out over Las Vegas. It is a mud-brown expanse of desert with craggy hills in the distance that has improbably filled up with mankind and its stuff. As the phone rang it didn't surprise me that Gaia would want to attack Vegas. It's all about excess. About man's domination of nature.

"You boys having fun?" she said as greeting.

"You might say that," I replied.

"What's going on, Nik?"

"I wasn't quite forthcoming with you on why we came up here," I said.

"Oh," she said flatly. I wished that I could see her, it would help me gauge the level of surprise and/or disappointment.

But I couldn't see her so I just told her everything. In detail. And then I apologized for the deception and tried to explain. "It's Chaosboy. I... he... The kid is dangerous in ways that are hard to explain. I thought maybe we could..." I trailed off with a heavy sigh and waited for her reply. It took a while for her to speak and in that time my stomach felt like it was falling out of my body.

"Why are you telling me this now?" she asked. Again no clues as to her emotional state, just straight to the practicalities.

I took a deep breath and sighed. "We need you. We need Lightningirl. There is—"

"No," she said cutting me off, her tone so flat that I knew it wasn't good. Our relationship had truly started when she had stopped being Lightningirl, had given up on it after the trauma of the Battle of Palo Verde. What had developed between us had been strictly q-morph free.

"They say it will go bad, really bad, without you," I said.

"Who is 'they'?" she asked.

I bit my lip before replying, sitting down on the big bed with a sigh. "Tom told me, but there are simulations that Byte did. I am sure—"

"Oh, so you and Toxicwasteman are on a first name basis now?"

"Licia, it's not like that. They know things we don't. Byte's simulations are eerily prescient. If they say we need you, I believe them."

There was silence on the other end of the phone. I could hear the sound of her pacing on her hardwood floors in her cabin that backs to the pine forest of Flagstaff.

"I need you, Licia," I said. The pacing stopped, but she didn't speak. "I am a better man with you, and a better Neutrinoman with Lightningirl. This is now about preserving innocent life. Please."

More silence and then she sighed. "I'll do this for you, Nik. Just this once."

"Thank you."

"I'll pack up and get headed towards you as quickly as I can," she said.

Now was the tough part. She wasn't going to like what was coming next. "There is a plane waiting for you at the Flagstaff airport."

"Oh?"

"And a car should be arriving at your house right about now."

I heard her walking on the floor again and then her sucking in a breath in surprise. "But I'll need some clothes... some..."

"There is a change of clothing in the car and toiletries too," I said.

"Nik, what the hell? This... I..."

"I know, honey. It's weird how good they are at this. Please just grab your purse, lock up the house, and get in the car. I'll see you in a few hours."

⸺

WHILE WE WAITED FOR LICIA, QUINN AND I POURED OVER the information on Gaia. It was a bit sketchy. We did know her powers revolved around the manipulation of earth. She could trigger an earthquake, cause a sinkhole, travel unseen underground.

There were a few blurry pictures of her too. A naked black woman looking over the destruction caused by La Conchita landslide in California. Or a blurry picture of the back of her in Sterling Heights, Michigan, after a sinkhole opened up in 2004. There were five of these in total. Images that might be her near recent natural disasters. The implication was that these disasters weren't exactly natural.

There was also a thick wad of paper outlining the simulations Byte had run—seeming endless data about actions, participants, and the odds of what would happen.

We were just digging into these when the door opened and Licia walked in. She had a keycard in her hand (I presume that was part of what was waiting for her in the car) and a confused look on her face.

I walked over and took in her in my arms. She let me, but didn't really hug me back. "Thank you for coming," I said.

She nodded and took her bag into the room I was using. I heard the door to the bathroom shut and the sound of water running.

Quinn gathered up the packet of simulation information and got up. "I think I'll go find another place to review these."

"No," I said. "I should look at them too."

Quinn smiled and looked towards the bedroom Licia had disappeared into. "Look, this is going take time. You and Licia have not seen much of each other of late. I am sure you need to catch up."

I was about to protest again when there was a knock on the door and someone said, "Room service."

Quinn and I looked at each other. We were both surprised. I walked over, opened the door, and a young man dressed in black and white rolled the cart it. On it was champagne on ice and meals for two.

I lifted the metal covers on the two plates. One had a grilled portabella, brown rice, and steamed vegetables. The other had some salmon but was mostly cheese.

It was clear this meal was for Licia and I and neither of us had ordered it. More prescient action by LoVE.

Quinn chuckled and dashed out the door. "Call me if you need me. Otherwise I'll see you in the morning."

I was about to protest, but the waiter was leaving.

"What do I owe?" I asked him.

"It's already been taken care of, sir," he said with a smile.

Of course it was. This entire event had been carefully arranged. I had to wonder what was coming next.

6 / IN THE DOG HOUSE

A RELATIONSHIP IS NEVER CONSTANT, ALWAYS CHANGING. Sometimes you are closer than you can imagine, thinking each other's thoughts. Sometimes things are awkward and it seems you hardly know the person.

Licia and I ate, mostly silently, at the suite's small round table overlooking Main Street and a slice of old Las Vegas. The sun was gone, leaving only a dirty orange glow to the west. The champagne sat in its ice unopened.

You have to remember, we were early in our relationship, one that only began after Licia told me no repeatedly. I was scared. I didn't want to lose her, but I knew what I knew. That this Gaia was a real threat. That we needed her.

And that's just the big picture. Zoom in and what I knew was that I needed her, too. So at war in me was the desire to do what I knew was right (try to stop Gaia) with the desperation to do anything at all to keep her in my life. Our relationship was untested, of unknown strength.

These things are delicate.

Licia was dressed in jeans and a khaki-colored short-sleeved shirt with her silky black hair pulled back. She's petite with moderate curves, and looking at her was a balm for that caricature of her that Quinn became on the drive up.

Sometimes it's honestly hard to look at her. Because she is beautiful, yes. Because I love her more than I can express, yes. But today because I was afraid of losing her to this need.

"Can we talk about this?" I asked.

She speared a piece of asparagus, popped it in her mouth, and nodded towards me. Meaning, *if you want to talk, you start it up, buddy.*

"I know you want out of the q-morph game. I know you are still recovering from what happened at Palo Verde, about what happened to Ben." Her eyes darkened and she looked down at her food. Ben was a guard she was friends with that died during that battle. And she had killed for the first time during it—to save me. I had a similar trauma from the Incident at Yellowstone. These kinds of things aren't dealt with easily.

I took a deep breath and sighed, pushing around the cheese left on my plate. "How can we stand by while innocent lives are on the line?"

Her brown eyes met mine and they were hard. "Nik, you are always going to have to try to save the world. I know that about you. I accept it. And I already agreed to help. Why are you going over this again? Besides, it's not really the point, is it?"

And there it was. I didn't really understand what was bothering her. Except it's clear that my lack of understanding was an additional layer of the irritation.

It's one of those moments in a relationship. Do you understand your love well enough to empathize with them? Can you put yourself in their shoes and get a glimpse of their world?

This is a very valuable skill in any relationship. Empathy matters. But we were still early on in our time together. Was I supposed to know her that well already?

She smiled at me, a weak little smile full of irony. She wiped her mouth with the white cloth napkin, slid her chair back on the beige carpet, got up, walked into one of the bedrooms, and closed the door.

———

IT WAS NOT THE ROMANTIC EVENING I HAD BEEN HOPING FOR. I slept on the big brown couch just in case Quinn came back. He did, at 4:00 a.m., reeking of alcohol and stumbling.

"Ohh... Poor Nik," he said in an exaggerated whisper. "No lovey-lovey for poor, poor Nik." He added an uncharacteristic giggle to the end.

I was irritated. You have to understand, I was sleeping on the couch and Quinn was very drunk and making a nuisance of himself. And for Quinn to be drunk he has to want to be drunk—he can easily adjust his biology and drink all day long and not feel a thing. So instead of studying the simulations he went out on the town and purposely got drunk—and God knows what else.

"Go to bed, Quinn," I said.

He slapped the papers with the simulations down on the dark wood coffee table. "Screwed, Nik-o. We are screwed."

I pushed myself into a sitting position and looked at Quinn. His handsome face showed clear signs of worry (and inebriation). Maybe the simulations were why he got drunk.

And then I was really mad. Not at Quinn, but at myself. I can have empathy in two seconds for my partner, but not for my lover? What the hell?

"Sit down," I said, indicating the overstuffed chair near the couch. "Explain it to me."

"Well..." he said, pointing at me in a very exaggerated fashion. "If this simulation stuff is good—and I know you believe it is—there is only one way to stop her and avoid disaster. Only one way, my nuclear friend, to avoid big disaster."

I was puzzled. "That doesn't sound so bad."

He laughed loudly, the sound of it bouncing around the suite. His laughter was too high pitched, too manic. I had never seen Quinn this out of sorts. I didn't like it. "The problem is," he said, leaning towards me, his eyes wide. "You will never do it. Not in million years."

"What, Quinn? What won't I do?"

"Kill her. The only way to stop her and big disaster is for you to kill her the moment you see her."

LICIA MADE QUINN COFFEE. HE DIDN'T NEED IT—HE COULD sober up in an instant if he wanted to. But I let it be. If Quinn "needed" coffee to get sober, then so be it.

She was dressed in a fluffy white robe with the Golden Nugget logo on it. Quinn's ranting woke her up. She found out what was going on and got all practical (she's very good at practical). She started the coffee and started digging through the printouts of the simulation data.

"He'll never do it," Quinn said with a slur. "And even if he did, it just makes it worse."

It was silent in the room for a while as Licia flipped through the papers scanning them rapidly. "Here it is," she said. "'Scenario 20a: Eliminate with extreme prejudice. Action: Neutrino must attack at first sight with a barrage of neutrino bolts. Result: 85% chance of Gaia's death, destruction averted. Long-Term Ramification: Chances of winning war are halved; we need Gaia's power long term.'"

Licia got up, poured three black coffees, gave one to Quinn, one to me, and sat down with the other. It was nearly 5:00 a.m. and I could see the sky starting to lighten just a touch outside.

"What do we do?" she asked. "Presuming these simulations are right, there must be something we can—"

Licia was cut off as all three of our phones chirped, signaling that text messages were received. The laptop, still sitting on the coffee table, then came to life. On it was Tom Tyree. For once he didn't have a grin on his face, but a deep frown.

"I'm glad you're awake," he said. "We know what Gaia's target is. You need to leave now if you have any chance of stopping her."

7 / TARGET: HOOVER DAM

I DROVE. QUINN WAS STILL TAKING HIS TIME SOBERING UP AND we didn't have a moment to spare.

"You two are adorable couple," he said from the backseat, his voice a bit slurred. "Make up, okay. What is old saying..." He trailed off, and I thought he might have dozed off or something, but about a minute later he finished. "A couple should never go into battle angry at each other. That's it."

The saying was about going to bed angry, of course, but Quinn's point was well taken.

"Is it Tom?" I asked, glancing at Licia sitting in the passenger's seat. "That I let him go? That I trust him on this?" We were out past the edge of Vegas and making the climb towards Boulder City. She was staring out the window as the desert whipped by in the yellow light of dawn. Just like I had been doing when Quinn had driven us to Vegas.

She sighed and glanced at me before staring back out at the desert. She was silent for a long time and I was about to open my mouth again when she said, "That is irritating and disturbing. The man is a psychopath. The man is using you—and now us. But no, that is not it."

I tried to engage her more, but it wasn't happening so I gave up and drove us to Hoover Dam as fast as I could.

THE HOOVER DAM. SEVEN HUNDRED TWENTY-SIX FEET TALL, 3,250,000 cubic yards of concrete. Holding back the Colorado River and sixteen million acre-feet of water. Providing electricity to Nevada, Arizona, and California. The Hoover Dam is an epic piece of human engineering, and I love epic pieces of human engineering.

Things like the Hoover Dam give me hope. Hope that we as a race can find ways to work with nature in ways that aren't so invasive and terrible for the planet. And, yeah, I get that the river isn't free and all, but it's better than choking the air with coal smoke.

The dam sits in a narrow river gorge carved by the Colorado River. And the Colorado is no slouch—it also made the Grand Canyon. It holds back Lake Mead, the largest reservoir in the country, when it's full.

This was Gaia's target. She wanted to destroy the dam and free the waters trapped in Lake Mead.

In 2005, when this happened, the bypass bridge over the river gorge was still under construction and traffic on US 93 went over the dam itself. Because of the early hour, there wasn't much traffic. We wound our way down through tight switchbacks carved into the reddish-brown rock of the canyon and onto the west edge of the dam. I stopped the car and got out.

"The Hammer?" Quinn asked from the backseat of the Focus. He had finally sobered up.

"Yes," I said.

Licia was out and looking around. We didn't know all that

much. Just that this was the target and Gaia was expected this morning.

The click-squish sound came from the car as Quinn transformed into The Hammer.

A couple cars stopped behind us and were honking. Several security guards were yelling at us and running our way.

The Hammer got out of the car and said, "Need steel." Quinn's already deep voice was an octave lower.

I guess I should take a moment and talk about q-morphs and the conservation of mass. Quinn weighed about 250 pounds, so when he transformed, he still weighed 250 pounds. So Sadie weighed 250 pounds, and even that petite, nightmare rendition of Licia he did weighed 250 pounds. He can't suddenly weigh something different unless he acquires or releases mass.

So when The Hammer got out of the car, he weighed 250 pounds.

You know what The Hammer looks like, right? All dark grey skin, flat features, huge chest, fists as big as your head. In most images of him he's covered in steel armor plates and weighs more like 350 or 400 pounds. That's why he asked about steel, he needed it to complete the transformation.

"Car?" he asked looking at my Ford Focus with its faded blue paint.

The Hammer also has a different personality than Quinn. His endocrine system and metabolism are significantly altered. He is constantly adrenalized and has epic amounts of energy (and needs epic amounts of food).

"No," I said and pointed him towards the steel guardrail along the road as I moved to intercept the guards. Licia was at the edge of the dam, tendrils of electricity starting to flow from the power lines above us to her outstretched left hand.

"Sir, you will have to..." the lead guard said. He was a grey-haired man with brown eyes. He trailed off when he noticed The Hammer and what he was doing with the guardrail.

It's that whole molecular manipulation thing. The Hammer had his hands on the guardrail, and the steel was flowing onto his body. By touching it, he was able to manipulate it at a molecular level, the molecules relocating to his chest, his arms, his forehead, his fists. It looked like the metal was liquid as it crawled all over his body. The metal was making a high-pitched groan as it flowed onto him.

"Do you know who I am?" I asked. I didn't have my hat or sunglasses on. I wanted to be recognized.

He and the sandy-haired guard next to him looked at me and the older one nodded.

"Good. I'm here because of a credible terrorist threat against the dam. I need you to initiate an evacuation and start any kind of disaster protocols you might have."

"Excuse me?" the sandy-haired one asked.

"There is a threat to the dam that could destroy it. We need to move fast. Evacuate. Warn everyone downstream."

"Sir, you'll have to move your car, or I'll have it towed," the older man said. Maybe it was just too much, but they didn't seem to be getting it.

"What now?" The Hammer asked as he came up next to me. He's about my height, six feet, but so much wider. He's strong as an ox and relatively quick on his feet. In a hand-to-hand battle between anything biological and The Hammer, well, The Hammer will win. And I mean anything—he could take on a rhinoceros, I'm sure of it.

"Block the traffic on the other end of the dam," I said to The Hammer. The guards were still talking, but I wasn't listening to them anymore.

The Hammer ran off, I could feel the vibration of his pounding feet through the asphalt. "And don't hurt anyone," I yelled.

"There she is," Licia yelled. Licia was standing on the low concrete wall that edges the sidewalk that goes across the dam. To her right was the visitors center with several floors of glass looking over the canyon and the damn. Right above her were high-tension power lines and she was starting to draw a thick bolt of electricity from it.

I ran over next to her. She put her right hand on my shoulder and began to pump electricity into me. It felt good to have her by my side again.

I didn't have time to appreciate the dam, the massive concave form of it holding back hundreds of feet of water, the generating station a U far below that hugged the bottom of the dam and the sides of the canyon. All off-white against the rough rocks. Clean, renewable energy and a stark emblem of mankind's manipulation of their environment.

I looked and could see a figure across the gorge standing on a rocky protrusion above the other side of the dam. I couldn't see her as well as Licia, but I could tell it was a woman with brown skin. She was naked and standing proud. Jena Grange. Gaia.

And suddenly I knew why Licia was upset with me. "I'm sorry I didn't tell you the truth about why we came up here."

She looked at me and smiled. I finally figured it out. It wasn't that I asked for her help or that I had this weird relationship with Tom Tyree. It was the most basic of things. I hadn't been honest with her.

"That's it. Right?" I asked.

The ground rumbled beneath us, rocks falling from the cliff Gaia was standing on. This wasn't the pounding of The Hammer's feet. This felt like an earthquake.

"Not now, dear," Licia said as she transformed into Lightningirl, her clothing burning off of her as her flesh transformed into blue-white swirls of her q-morph form. "We've got a mission."

INTERLUDE 2: WHAT A WOMAN WANTS

Not surprisingly, Licia and I worked well together as we built the greenhouse. I am physically stronger, but she has a better eye for detail and more patience with the small stuff.

We've got the steel frame in place and are getting ready to start installing the windows. It's a much bigger greenhouse than our old one. It will be nice and will let us grow more of our own food.

The hot sun was beating down from a clear blue sky. It was a lovely summer day in the high desert. We're both standing off a few paces, eyeing our work, taking a break.

The rolling high desert hills framed the greenhouse and we were far enough away from I-17 to the west that it was dead quiet.

"So..." I began, my brain still full of the past and the story I had been writing that morning. "Honesty. Is that what a woman wants most?"

She gave me an appraising look. "We're about to fight Gaia, right?" she asked.

I nodded.

"Hell of a time for a realization," she said, a smile on her face.

"Quinn said we shouldn't go into battle angry." I said it like a joke, but her smile disappeared and her face darkened.

"Well... is it?" I asked, trying to change the subject. "Is honesty the most important thing?"

A slight breeze came up and was licking at the sweat on my skin. It felt good. I had nothing but shorts and shoes on, as usual, so I could absorb as much UV radiation as possible.

"It's not that simple," Licia said.

"Well, explain it to me."

She smiled and shrugged. "Think of it like baking bread."

I wasn't much of a baker, but I nodded for her to continue.

"Honesty is like the yeast. If you don't have any yeast, your bread will turn into a dense, inedible block of wheat. Yeast makes the bread rise. Yeast makes bread, bread."

I pursed my lips and nodded, thinking about it. "So yeast is the most important ingredient in bread as honesty is the most important ingredient in a relationship."

She shook her head and sighed. "No. You need all the ingredients. Leave out water and you still don't have bread. Leave out the passion in a relationship and there is no relationship."

I love my wife. How much I can't even convey to you. We have managed to stick together through so much. Our lives have changed radically many times. She even puts up with my dredging up the past and my philosophical meanderings.

"So it's kind of like alchemy?" I asked.

She smiled and nodded. "Exactly. Don't get me wrong, honesty is a basic requirement, but it takes passion and commitment and trust and patience and so much more to make it work."

"So you like honesty," I said, a silly grin creeping onto my face.

Her brow furrowed as her eyes searched mine, but she said, "Yes, I do."

"Great, then let me be honest with you about something very serious."

"Okay..."

"I'm horny," I said with a big grin. "How about we take a break and—"

She sighed and rolled her eyes, stopping me.

"Too much honesty?" I asked.

She laughed and nodded. "We've got work to do." She walked back to our construction site. I gladly followed.

8 / GAIA

STANDING THERE ON THE EDGE OF THE HOOVER DAM, THE ground rumbling beneath us, we didn't speak. We just acted. Licia transformed into Lightningirl. I transformed into Neutrinoman. Our clothes burning away and dropping to the ground.

She hopped on my back and I flew us across the river gorge toward the salmon colored outcrop of stone above the east end of the dam.

Despite our time apart, despite Licia's fear of flying, we knew what to do. I missed her acutely in that moment despite her proximity—it had been too long since we had been Neutrinoman and Lightningirl together.

I was a contained nuclear reaction, swirling motes of yellow with neutrino jets shooting out of my palms and feet to power our flight.

Lightningirl was a contained electrical reaction, blue-white, her left hand outstretched while she continued to pull electricity from the Hoover Dam in the form of a coruscating lightning bolt. Her hair was a halo of sparking electricity around her, and with her feminine curves she looked the part of a goddess.

Where our bodies met, they did their dancing exchange of energy, my yellow to her blue-white, the two of us together making a whole that was more than the sum of its parts.

As I flew, I noticed a few things.

The Hammer bodily moving a car on the far end of the dam below the rock. He punched the tire, blowing it out and made sure the car couldn't move. The road down to the dam had been carved into the rock so the outcropping Gaia stood on rose as a cliff about fifty feet above him.

It was early, but a few cars and trucks were backed up trying to get across the dam. There were guards on that side too, wisely keeping their distance from The Hammer. In fact, there were people running away from The Hammer (and the dam), which was a good thing.

I heard and saw out of the corner of my eye a helicopter flying high above us. It seemed too early for a tour, but I didn't think anything of it.

And then there was Gaia. She stood there calmly, her head turning to watch The Hammer below and then Lightningirl and me flying towards her.

We arrived and landed on the stone near her. She was still calm, which was beginning to worry me. Lightningirl hopped off my back and the three of us stood there staring at each other.

It was a spectacular spot. The off-white expanse of the Hoover Dam squatting in the deep canyon, its concave surface holding back the vast blue of Lake Mead. Seven hundred feet below us, the Colorado River. Dark blue skies above us, slowly lightening as the sun rose.

Gaia was about 5'5" with brown skin and long, curly black hair that fell across her shoulders and down her back. She had full lips and a wide nose showing her African heritage. She was completely nude. Like most of us transforming q-morphs, there is no costume that can survive what she can do. She had wide hips and large breasts. She wasn't fat, but she wasn't skinny either. She looked like an ancient carving of a fertility goddess. She had the kind of body suited to childbirth.

"Hi," I said, filling the silence. "I'm Neutrinoman, this is Lightningirl. You must be Gaia."

Her brown eyes, deep and intense, turned on me.

"You are the one that stopped the meteor," she said. She had a British accent, not cockney, more upper crust, like she came from a wealthy family.

"Yes," I said with a nod and a smile.

"I hate you," she said, her tone flat.

Lightningirl had stopped drawing power from the high-tension power lines and had tamped down her electrical reaction. She was still a swirl of blue-white electricity, but not as intimidating as when she is fully powered. I banked down my nuclear reaction too. We were just having a conversation. I had, obviously, rejected the strategy of killing her on sight.

"I'm sorry," I said. "Have I done something to harm you?"

"You stopped that meteor," she said, her lips twisted in a bitter frown.

I just stood there, my mouth moving. I had no clue as to why that would upset her.

"You mean you wanted the meteor to strike the earth?" Licia asked.

"Yes," she said. "Mankind is a disease. Mankind must be stopped. I must stop it."

─────

BACK THEN, IF YOU WERE TALKING ABOUT GAIA AND IF YOU were being generous, you would use words like "passionate," "dedicated," and "uncompromising." If you weren't being generous you would use words like "crazy" and "radical."

Her tone as we talked was calm. Way too calm, really. Her arguments were unfailingly logical. Her conclusions were... well, they were scary as hell.

"Disease?" I asked. "How is mankind a disease?"

"It spreads across the planet unchecked," Gaia said, sweeping her hand to encompass the dam and all its support structures. "It uses resources for individual gain without thought to the whole or to the planet. Mankind is selfish and gluttonous, taking much more from the Earth than it needs. This is the behavior of a disease. The behavior of a virus or a cancer so virulent it will foolishly kill its host in the name of its own greed."

"Oh," I said. How the hell could I counter that? She wasn't exactly wrong. I just happened to value human life too much to go there.

"Mankind is a mess," Licia said. "I will give you that. But things are getting better."

"Better?" Gaia asked, turning her gaze on Licia.

"Yes, better. Look at this country a hundred years ago. African Americans were much worse off, not treated as equals. The plight of women has also improved radically—we're not expected to just raise a family anymore. We can go out into the world and make our own way, although it is maddening we don't have a ratified Equal Rights Amendment. The Clean Air Act of 1970 did much to curtail pollution and the Endangered Species Act of 1973 helped with extinction of our animals."

"And yet there is an island of garbage in the Pacific," Gaia said. "Species are still becoming extinct all the time. Poverty is rampant in the third world, and first-world countries like this one do so little to help. Global warming is denied by the western powers despite mounting evidence."

"But it is getting better," I said. I was amazed at how well educated Licia was on this topic. I had no idea. "The Gates Foundation is putting billions towards dealing with problems like malaria and trying to pull the poorest nations out of poverty." And I only knew that because Bill Gates was the richest person in the world and even I hear news about him.

"Though we fight, our world is getting more civilized," Licia said. "You don't have to do this."

"We need you," I added.

Her brow furrowed as her deep brown eyes searched mine. "You need me?" she asked.

As we talked, I noticed a few things. First, she was completely unashamed of her nudity. I really envied that. Maybe she grew up someplace less uptight about such things than Arizona. Second, her feet were buried in solid rock up to her ankles. No sign of the rock being disturbed whatsoever. It was like she was part of the rock. In fact, the lower half of her calves appeared to be sandstone.

"Yes," I said. "We need you. Humans aren't perfect, but we are getting better. We are trying to improve. We need you to help us..." I trailed off. We needed her to help save the human race, but she didn't seem to be very much interested in that.

"To save the planet," Licia interjected, phrasing it in a way she might actually be able to hear. "Neutrinoman is famous now. He can help get you a forum to speak on these issues. He can get you in with the Gates Foundation to see if they can help address your concerns."

My mouth dropped open. She was committing me to a lot, but something clicked then. I *was* famous. I *had* a forum. Shouldn't I be doing something about it? Wasn't poverty, human rights, and climate change worthy of more attention? "Yes," I said. "I will do anything I can to help address these issues. You can join us, Gaia. You can help us and we can help you."

"But..." Gaia began, her eyes looking towards the northwest, towards Las Vegas. "That place is such a blight. Such an affront to Mother Earth. I must strike against it. I must..."

Lightningirl and I were getting through. I knew it. I could see it in her eyes. But then along came The Hammer.

9 / PUTTING THE HAMMER DOWN

IF YOU THINK OF THE HAMMER AS A ROIDED UP FOOTBALL player with way too much testosterone flowing through his veins, you are pointed in the right direction, but you are under the mark by quite a bit. He's all that and much more.

While we had been talking, he had been acting. Blocking the east end of the dam and then running to the west end and chasing people off. The Hammer is not dumb, he's just filled with so much fight that he often misses the obvious. When he was on the west side of the dam he looked across and spotted us up on the cliff. He saw Gaia. He knew she was dangerous. He acted.

"Please," I said to Gaia. "Let's leave this place. Let's talk. I promise I will help you address these concerns. I..."

I heard him grunt as The Hammer finally found a way up the cliff. He had to go up the road to the east a ways, find a slope not too steep to climb, and come up the back side of the rock.

When I saw him, his head was down and he was running hard with a branch of some sort of bush sticking out of his mouth. That's the other thing about The Hammer, to keep that energy going he eats anything organic he finds in his path.

"No!" I shouted, holding my hands up and running towards him. But it was too late to reason with him. There was not enough time for my intent to get through his brain. I ran towards him intending to push him out of the way, but he threw me aside.

Licia threw her left hand back and a lightning bolt leapt from the high-tension power line to her left hand, and from her right hand it spiked out to The Hammer. It wasn't a lot of electricity, she was just trying to get his attention.

But that wasn't enough either, his momentum shot him towards the wide-eyed Gaia. But when he should have connected with her, she was gone and The Hammer went flying over the cliff towards the Colorado River seven hundred feet below.

⸺

I WASN'T HAPPY WITH THE HAMMER, BUT I WENT AFTER HIM anyway. I wasn't thinking, just reacting. After taking a single step, I was flying after him, yellow neutrino jets firing out of my feet and palms.

Once I got over the outcrop we had been on, I could see that he had cleared the service road and was falling down the gorge. I spotted him when he bounced off the side of the canyon.

This was a fool's errand, really. It takes all of five seconds to fall seven hundred feet, and I was about a second behind. That bounce, though, helped. It slowed him down just a touch.

I flew hard and fast, and by the time he was halfway down, I had a hold of his hand. He had this wide-eyed look on his flat face. He was afraid. The Hammer can take a lot of damage, but slamming into the ground at 140 miles per hour would probably cause him some issues, maybe even do enough damage fast enough so he wouldn't be able to heal himself.

Not that I could stop him from slamming into the ground, not at the pace we were going. What I could do was slow him down. So as I clung to his arm, I pointed my feet and my free hand down and put out as much thrust as I could with the neutrino jets. The Hammer screamed.

There was a reason Quinn was my partner. His ability to control his body at a molecular level made him able to heal quickly. To heal from radiation. He wasn't immune, it was just that he could take a good amount of it without any lasting damage.

When I grabbed him, my reaction was hot. I was slowing him down, but I was burning his hand at the same time, at a rate his body couldn't quite keep up with. It hurt, thus the deep-throated scream of The Hammer as we fell.

At the bottom of the dam was a U-shaped, white-roofed building that hugged the downstream end of the dam and ran along both sides of the river. This was the roof of the hydroelectric generation station. Water from Lake Mead was funneled through turbines here to generate electricity. Water flows out the bottom of it into the river gorge.

I had slowed us down. Not completely, but enough to make the landing survivable. We slammed into that white roof hard and kept going.

The generator room was huge. About ten stories tall with a long row of massive round turbines. We crashed through the roof, which was reinforced with steel girders, and slammed to the floor below, debris from the roof raining down upon us.

The floor was concrete and I landed first, cratering it out a bit. The Hammer landed on top of me.

Not a pleasant landing, but I've had much worse.

There were large walkways to either side and a few hard-hat-wearing workers were staring at us. I didn't blame them. It's not that often you see two superheroes crashing through your roof.

We got lucky in that on the far end of the station there were no generators for us to land on. Only hard floor.

"Thanks," The Hammer grunted as he got up and brushed

himself off. I could see his hand and forearm repairing the damage from the radiation.

"Sure," I said, standing and looking up through the hole in the roof.

We were grinning at each other. In truth these kinds of things are exciting. A near brush with death, a daring save you can walk away from. I was starting to feel better about the day. And I had always wanted to take a tour of the dam, not that this was the way I imagined it. I loved these kinds of big engineering projects. It's what led me to become a janitor at Palo Verde—I really just wanted an inside look. I wanted to learn how it worked. And that simple curiosity led to the accident at Palo Verde on the day the cosmic rays hit that turned me into Neutrinoman.

That's when the floor started to shake underneath us and I could hear rocks striking the roof above. A few came through the hole we had made and fell on us.

"Oh no," The Hammer said.

"I don't think this is over," I said.

I looked through the hole above us. I could see clear blue sky, still slowly lightening as the sun rose, and then I saw... Well, I didn't believe what I saw, but it looked like a flash of rock framed in the blue sky. The rock looked like a clenched fist, and then it was gone, and then the whole building shook hard.

I looked around and at one end of the room there was an observation deck and a group of tourists there gawking at us.

I looked at The Hammer. "Get this place evacuated and get out of here. I'm going to go see what this is."

The Hammer nodded and started running to a set of stairs that went up to the observation deck.

"And be gentle," I yelled after him.

I looked up and saw that huge fist-shaped rock pass over and the whole room shook again. People were screaming and a high-pitched alarm went off.

INTERLUDE 3: AN INTERVIEW REQUEST

Licia had a puzzled look on her face as she walked out of our little adobe casita and towards the greenhouse we were building. She had two glasses of iced tea in one hand and a plate of cheese in the other. I could smell the cheese from fifty yards away and it made my stomach grumble.

I was obsessed with cheese and had an extraordinary sense of smell because of the rat that bit me the day of the accident, the day I became what I am.

There are always three elements for those of us that transformed into q-morphs. For me it was a rat, endowing me with an excellent sense of smell and an everlasting need for cheese. For Licia it was a raven and giving her excellent eyesight and an unerring sense of direction.

I was glad to see her. It was just past noon and hot as hell. Construction is hungry work, but the puzzled look on her lovely face gave me pause.

"What's up?" I asked when she got close.

She handed me the plate and one of the glasses of tea and sat down on the flagstone floor, but she didn't speak.

I sat next to her, taking a long drink and then popping a piece of Munster in my mouth.

"That was Diane Madison on the phone," she said quietly.

I was in mid-swallow and choked on the cheese, coughing hard.

"She wants to interview you," she said when I had cleared my throat. "Actually, she wants to interview both of us."

Diane Madison. The woman who had outed our identities. The woman that had inserted herself in our business every chance she got. The woman who had... Well, we're not to that part of the story yet, but suffice it to say we had reason to be wary of Diane Madison.

"You told her no, right?" I asked. "Preferably loudly and then hung up on her."

Licia slowly shook her head. "I told her yes."

"What!" I stood and began pacing the floor of the greenhouse. We had the main posts in and had started on the glass roof. "Why? Why would you do that?"

Licia took a deep breath and slowly sighed. "For you, hon." She added a small smile, her eyes tracking me as I paced. "You said it was time that we have more of a life, aren't cooped up here all the time. Isn't that what you want?"

I stopped in front of her. Her expression was still an odd one. Part shock, part determination. Her brow was furrowed as she stared up at me, her lips forming the barest of smiles, her eyes wide.

"Diane is doing a segment in her 'Where Are They Now?' series about the war. She's got two presidents booked and General Markus. She's calling all of us q-morphs that survived."

I sat back down on the cool stone next to my wife. "Why would she be doing that?"

"She tied herself to you early on," Licia said. "Her star was hitched to your wagon when it all went to hell in the end. When we had to sign the Q-Morph Accord of 2020 and were all gotten out of the way, she went down too."

I took another bite of cheese and ate it slowly. Diane was in it for herself, and knowing that made me feel better.

"America loves their heroes," Licia said.

"But they love to see them fall even more," I added. We had said this to each other many times when things had gone to hell.

"I reminded Diane of that," Licia said. "And you know what she said?"

I shook my head.

"That what America loves even more is to see their heroes redeemed. She thinks it's time, Nik. She thinks it's all because of these little books you are writing."

I bristled at the adjective "little" being associated with my writing. It didn't feel "little" at all, although they were fairly short, so maybe that is what she meant. But I let it pass. "But what if she doesn't behave? What if she screws us over again?"

A wicked smile played on Licia's lips. "She'll be good," she said.

"How do you know?"

"I told her if she wasn't, she would have me to deal with. That I would wait until it was a dark and stormy night in LA when lightning rained down on the city. And a stray bolt of lightning would stab out from her TV or a wall socket. That that lightning would kill her, and that lightning would be me."

It was suddenly quiet around us. The heat of the high desert day had driven all the animals underground. The air was still, and the sun hung in a clear blue sky.

"Seriously?" I asked.

She laughed. "Seriously, although my tone was much more menacing when I told her."

I wanted to ask her if she would really do something like that, but then stopped myself. I really didn't want to know the answer.

She grabbed my hand. "You want more of a life, we need the public to remember us, to remember all that we did. We need her and she needs us."

I nodded, feeling my stomach tighten at the thought.

"Besides, if she screws us in the edit you have your own forum now. You can write about the interview, tell the truth about it. It'll be okay."

I nodded, but I wasn't sure.

"So," Licia continued. "I guess we need to get Agent Peters out here."

Agent Peters is with Homeland Security. He's what I affectionately think of as our "landlord." He's really more like our "guard" or "warden," keeping us happy so we stay on our reservation and don't bother the people now that the war is over.

And yes, I used the word "reservation." I'm from Arizona, I've been to the Navajo and Hopi reservations numerous times. I don't use that word lightly. With the Quantum Metamorph Accord of 2020, all of us surviving q-morphs were basically restricted to our own plot of land.

We are not living in the third-world conditions of the real reservations, but we are isolated and restricted here. We are treated differently because of who we are. Our plight is not anywhere near as extreme, but there are parallels.

"Well," I said with a smile, pointing up. "I know how to get his attention."

Licia smiled and nodded. We wrapped up our work and headed towards our launch pad, an area of flagstones near the high-tension power lines that run near our home. We had been seeing Agent Peters a lot more. I would fly us up into orbit every week or two where I could soak up some nice radiation from the sun. And every time Agent Peters would be here when we got down, questioning our unauthorized use of powers, making us fill out a ton of paperwork.

After we had transformed into our q-morph selves, Licia standing on my feet, her arms around my neck, I said, "Thank you." I would never have agreed to an interview with Diane Madison myself. I needed the push. "I think this could help."

She smiled and held me tightly as we soared into the air.

When I flew up out of the generating station, I couldn't believe my eyes. And, frankly, I wouldn't expect you to believe what I write here, but you've all seen the videos and pictures shot that day. It was early, but a few tourists did capture some images, and someone in that helicopter had a camera recording the whole thing.

What I saw was a seven-hundred-foot-tall rock giant. A colossus. Gaia, fully transformed and mad as hell.

That rock outcropping we had talked to the humanoid Gaia on was the head, its features roughly that of a woman, her rough features that of Jena Grange. The fist I had seen from below was the left fist of the rock giant, and as I flew up, that fist flew past me and slammed into the dam again, taking out a chunk of the top of the dam and throwing debris into Lake Mead.

The colossus Gaia appeared to be pinned by the dam. Her left side was in the open on the downstream side of the dam while her right side was on the upstream side of the dam.

It was unbelievable.

I flew up to the height of the dam and out of reach of the giant, my mouth hanging open. I mean, this was not something I had ever imagined seeing. And as I watched, the colossus began to look more like her human self as rock fell away. The chest pinned by the dam, one breast visible. The hips forming down the rock gorge. A long leg and foot now stomping on the transformer station at the bottom of the river gorge just downstream from the generating station. Rocks fell. Sparks flew. And a deep shout of rage escaped Gaia's rock lips. The sound was like rock against rock and I could literally feel it when the sound hit me.

Mother Nature was angry. She didn't like this dam. She was going to destroy it.

As I gawked, as I tried to get my mind in gear, tried to figure out how to stop Gaia, Lightningirl acted.

Lightning stabbed out from behind me and struck the rock giant. I looked back and saw Lightningirl in full goddess mode standing on top of the visitor's center, the ornate patinaed copper roof behind her, a hundred feet of windows below her, the main tower of it rising out of the rocky canyon all glass and copper accents.

She was drawing a large bolt of electricity from the high-tension power lines to her left hand and lightning was arcing from her right hand and striking the giant. She was fully powered, tiny bolts of electricity sparking off her swirling blue/white form, her electric hair haloed around her head, her hair snapping and sparking all around her face.

It was like the Goddess of the Earth was fighting the Goddess of Electricity.

I flew over to the roof and landed next to Lightningirl.

"I'm going to kill Quinn," she shouted over the crackling noise of the lightning bolts. "How do we stop her?"

She shot a bolt of electricity into my back. It's intense, it hurts, but it also feels good. There is something about our powers that are complementary. She can strengthen me with her electricity and I can strengthen her with my radiation. It's why we work so well together.

I started firing neutrino bolts at Gaia, yellow balls of coruscating neutrino energy leaping from my palms. About the size of a baseball, they fly straight and true and explode on impact.

I felt bad about doing it. I honestly didn't want to hurt her, but I didn't want her to destroy the dam, to send all that water rushing down the Colorado River towards Lake Mohave, which it would probably overrun, sending another wave of water farther down the river.

The area is sparsely populated. Below Lake Mohave is Laughlin on the Nevada side and Bullhead City on the Arizona side. Laughlin is kind of like a mini Las Vegas, with casinos lining the Colorado River. They would be decimated.

Farther down the river is Lake Havasu and then Yuma.

The desert southwest uses so much of the Colorado River that it is barely a trickle by the time it reaches Yuma and crosses into Mexico. It doesn't even make it all the way to the Gulf of Mexico anymore.

And maybe this was just the first dam on the Colorado River that Gaia was going to target. Maybe she would take out Lake Mead and Lake Havasu and then go upstream and take out Glen Canyon Dam and drain Lake Powel, which would send a torrent of water through the Grand Canyon.

So I shot neutrino bolts at the rock giant pinned by the dam. She kept pounding at it with her left fist and then her right. Breaking through the top of the dam, the remnants of the road falling into the lake. Starting at the top, each blow knocked away a part of the dam. Left right, left right, her rhythmic beating quickly destroying the dam where she pounded, throwing debris down the canyon or back into the river.

The lake's water levels were low, the top of the dam a hundred feet or so above the water, so she could fully use both fists in aid in the destruction. Her position pinned by the dam gave her perfect leverage. Concrete flying out with each blow, cracks radiating, the sound of it like small explosions each time the colossus's fist struck. We could feel the vibration of it under our feet.

She didn't waste any energy on the intake tower rising up out of the lake even though it was within reach. She was focused on the dam, beating a chunk of it away with every blow.

The loud sirens continued to scream and I saw that they were finally evacuating, people spilling out of the visitor's center below us and running up the road away from the dam.

My bolts had an effect. Where they hit Gaia, rock would explode, but soon it would be replaced by other rock. On my second attempt, a few bolts hit her hand taking out the top third of it. But it wasn't effective, soon rock flowed down her arm and the thumb and index finger were recreated.

I landed some bolts on her left elbow, same effect. She would just draw more rock from the cliff and repair the damage. This caused the cliff to erode back behind her.

My bolts seemed to cause her pain. Each time one landed, that grinding rock-on-rock scream would escape her, drowning out the drone of the siren.

I stopped firing at her. It wasn't working.

Lightningirl, though, was getting somewhere. At first her light-ning didn't seem to have any effect at all. She struck Gaia's fist and arm and chest and hip and leg to no effect. The giant just seemed to absorb the electricity.

But then she landed a bolt on the giant's head right between the eyes and that got its attention.

The pounding of the fists stopped and Gaia turned her gaze to us. Her rock face now looked very much like her human face and she looked mad.

"Uh oh," I said.

Gaia cocked her left arm back—and I must remind you it was over two hundred feet long, so it was quite the display. She cocked her arm back, and instead of slamming her fist into the dam, she swung it towards us with it ending up pointed directly at us, fingers splayed. A boulder flew from her hand right at us. I grabbed Lightningirl and started flying us up just as the boulder hit where we had been standing.

The roof of the visitor's center exploded around us, debris flying everywhere.

As I flew us, Lightningirl didn't stop. She kept targeting the giant's head with her lightning bolts. I had grabbed her from behind and had both of my arms around her. My flight was wobbly using just my feet and I quickly landed her on the now abandoned dam not far from the visitor's center.

"I'm fine," Lightningirl shouted. "Target her head, right between the eyes. There's something there."

The Hoover Dam is forty-five feet wide at the top and over six hundred feet wide at the bottom. Gaia had done a tremendous amount of damage the short time she had been beating on the structure. She had opened up a gap on the Arizona side almost down to the water line, the break in it making it clear how the dam widens the lower you go.

Even with all that concrete it was clear that given even a little more time, she would work her way down to the water level if not completely destroying the structure.

The man-made dam was strong, but it appeared that the earth goddess was stronger.

Gaia was cocking her arm back again to launch another boulder at us as I took flight. I didn't love the idea of leaving Lightningirl, but I knew her capabilities. She was in full-on Goddess of Electricity mode—she could take care of herself.

I flew hard and fast just downstream of Gaia away from her swinging arm. I didn't fire, I looked. I wanted to see what Lightningirl had been referring too.

Right in the middle of the rock giant's forehead, right between the eyes, was a darker-colored spot. The head of this thing was over one hundred feet tall, and this brown spot was only about a foot tall. At first it looked like some random aberration of the stone, but as I flew closer, I saw what it was. I saw a face.

———

Jena Grange can manipulate the earth. That is her power. So this rock giant, this colossus that had formed, that was pinned by the Hoover Dam, was controlled by Jena, really was Jena. That face I saw was the human in the giant. She was still physically there, still physically part of it, still flesh and blood.

This is why the giant reacted when the lightning struck her there. By the time I had the realization, I was almost upon her. Gaia had just hurled another boulder at Lightningirl, but I wasn't aware of that at the time. I was focused on this tiny face buried in the rock of this huge giant. I was trying to decide what to do.

I didn't want to kill Jena but her actions were not acceptable. I ended up taking precious moments to ponder this as I flew towards her. It wasn't long, a second or so, but it was long enough so that I didn't have any maneuvering room. I was going to run right into that huge rock head.

So I used my final moments to adjust my trajectory and slammed right into the middle of the giant's forehead, right where Jena's head was embedded in the rock.

I didn't explode, like I had done with the meteor, I just slammed into the rock hard and then I was falling with rock, dirt, and boulders all around me, having no idea what was going on.

11 / GOODBYE FRYING PAN, HELLO FRYER

TUMBLING... DISORIENTED... BOUNCING BETWEEN ROCKS LIKE I was the ball in a pinball machine. As I tumbled, I tried to see light, but my vision was obscured, everything a gray haze around me. It took me a moment to realize water was falling on me and turning to steam, which is why I couldn't see.

And I could hardly think. The blows from the rocks didn't really damage me in my neutrino form, but the painful jolts kept me from thinking clearly.

It was only seconds, but then, through the mist, I saw lightning, a small tendril of it stabbing through the fog. I flew hard towards it and was soon out of the jumble of rocks and water as they tumbled down the side of the canyon and fell on top of the generator station.

When I had struck the colossus's head, it had fallen apart, like a puppet with its strings cut. All the rock that had moved, that had formed the legs, chest, arms, and head of Gaia, fell. It left a gap around the eastern edge of the dam, like a very badly receding gumline. Water was spilling over the gap, a huge torrent from the lake suddenly draining into the river below.

It was a massive waterfall, strangely beautiful.

I landed on the dam next to Lightningirl. "Thanks," I said.

"Anytime," she replied with a smile. The bolt arcing from the power lines to her hand had stopped. "Generator's out," she said.

It wasn't a surprise. Much of what had been Gaia had fallen on the generating station.

I looked back to the dam, the gap went about five feet below the water line. That meant the lake was about to go down by five feet and that all that water was going to hit Lake Mohave. I was hopeful that word had gotten out, that they had opened their flood gates. That the lake was being evacuated and that they could handle all that water.

I felt a thump, thump through the cement below my feet and had a bad moment. I was worried that Gaia was back, but I turned and saw The Hammer running from the visitor's center towards us.

The visitor's center was in shambles, the roof ripped off by the boulder Gaia had thrown at us. A few people were running out of it and away from the dam.

"What did I miss?" The Hammer asked.

"A seven-hundred-foot-tall rock giant," I said.

The expression on The Hammer's flat face was hard to read. It was a strange combination of disappointment and awe, with maybe a touch of fear.

"I think we're going to be okay," Lightningirl said. "Not great, but okay."

The waterfall was still going, a brief Niagara Falls in the Arizona desert. It was going to take quite some time for all that water to drain, but the dam was intact, Gaia was gone, and we had *kinda* saved the day. Well, let's put it this way: it could have been much worse.

"Yeah," I said with a smile. "I think we are. The dam gets thicker as you go down, there is no way that—"

A sharp bang both heard and felt through my feet stopped me short. I looked over at the dam and saw that more of the generating station's roof had collapsed and black smoke was roiling out.

"Oh no," The Hammer said. "You spoke too quick."

I smelled burning diesel and melted plastic. That first bang was followed by a much larger one, the dam moving below our feet, a blossom of yellow flame escaping the generating station six hundred feet below as more of the roof collapsed.

"This is not good," I said.

Lightningirl turned to The Hammer and said, "Unless you can fly, you best get off this dam right now."

You didn't have to tell him twice. The Hammer headed west, the thumping of his feet rapidly retreating.

I leaned over and looked at the dam, at the ragged V-shaped gap where Gaia had been beating on it, where water was spilling out. The line wasn't sharp, all crumbly edges with small cracks radiating out from it in all directions.

Gaia had been banging on the dam from both sides and had weakened it significantly, and the exploding power station had just made it worse.

As I looked, I heard a different kind of cracking sound. This one not as loud and much sharper. As I watched, the edges of the gap crumbled and it got bigger, especially at the bottom, the pressure of the lake and the water flowing rapidly, increasing the damage, the water flowing faster and getting stronger.

"Oh, shit!" I said.

"You've got to do something," Lightningirl said as the sharp cracking sound continued.

"What the hell can I do?"

"You have to do something," she said again.

"What!?"

We were a little freaked... Okay, a *lot* freaked out. This whole trip was supposed to be about having a conversation with Chaosboy, maybe bringing him in. But instead we were overseeing what was looking like the destruction of the Hoover Dam.

Not really how I saw this little "off book" adventure going.

Lightningirl looked at the lake spread out behind us. A blue expanse of water as far as the eye could see. She then looked down the deep and narrow river gorge. She then looked at me.

She was opening her mouth to say something when we were rocked by a third explosion from the generating station. The loud bang of the explosions was accompanied by even louder cracking from the dam.

It was starting to sound like thin ice when you walk on it. A sharp crack like gunfire that makes your heart race.

"Find a narrow area in the canyon," she shouted, pointing downstream. "Blow it to hell. Do something to slow this water down."

As if on cue, the cracking became loud and continuous and the dam shook beneath us. The small waterfall was getting bigger faster, the water pushing its way through the damaged dam.

With a flash of light, Lightningirl was gone and I was left there alone on the dam as it started to give way.

INTERLUDE 4: THE FUTURE

When we came down from orbit, Agent Peters and several other agents from Homeland Security were there. They stood stiffly in the desert sun dressed in their dark suits and sunglasses with a black SUV on our barely passable road. They looked like they stepped out of a *Men in Black* movie.

"This is becoming excessive," Peters said in lieu of a greeting. Peters is not a tall man, with short sandy hair and a rapidly receding hairline.

Licia and I had gone into our tin shed, transformed back to our biological bodies and put our clothing on. He had been out here regularly lately and each time he became grumpier.

"You are in clear violation of the agreement you signed," he added, mopping at his forehead with a handkerchief.

"What are you going to do?" I asked. "Throw us in a deep, dark hole and throw away the key?"

I didn't like Peters and he didn't like me. It was the nature of the relationship.

"Now, boys," Licia said with a disarming smile, "let's talk about this civilly, over iced tea."

She took Agent Peters's arm and escorted him and the other agents into the house. She sat with him at our small table in our sun-drenched kitchen with fresh wildflowers in a vase and windows all around. She served iced tea and cookies. She smiled and was charming. She cheerfully filled out the paperwork and made our jaunts into orbit sound like the most reasonable thing.

Agent Peters softened under the onslaught, but it wasn't like the first few times. This was obviously becoming a bigger issue.

And then she told him we had accepted an interview with Diane Madison in a month.

"No," he said flatly.

"Come again?" I said.

"No interviews," he said, his pale grey eyes connecting with mine. "It is against policy at this time."

"I don't care," I said.

Peters pursed his lips and folded his arms across his chest. This place is in some ways like a reservation or a prison, but in other ways it is not. We are superheroes. If we are dead set on something, they will have to go to extraordinary measures to stop us. I didn't think they were willing, seeing how we were insurance policies just in case our powers were ever needed again.

"Gentlemen," Licia said, her light tone slicing through the tension. "There must be a way. Contact Diane Madison and her producers, Agent Peters. This piece will be good PR for all of us."

The discussion went several more rounds with Peters saying "no" in several different ways, and me saying "try to stop me," and Licia trying to keep it reasonable.

When the agents left, we still hadn't come to an agreement. As soon as they walked out of the house, her smile was gone. "I hope this is worth it," she said.

"You set up this interview."

"You know what I mean, Nik. You want things to change, you

want a future where we can move around with some freedom. That is why I agreed to the interview. For you."

I sighed and rubbed at my face. Peters always wore me out. "I hope it is worth it too," I said.

I wanted change, that much was true. But I've been around long enough to know that the change you get is not often the change you envisioned.

SPRING 2005, COLORADO RIVER, NEVADA/ARIZONA BORDER

I FLEW HARD AND FAST—AND YES, THAT MEANS I WAS USING the infamous butt-thruster. After I stumbled into the ungraceful method of flight when battling the missile the aliens fired at Palo Verde, the military had me practice it. A lot. But the practice didn't make it look any less silly. With my legs drawn up against my abdomen and a huge yellow jet coming out of my ass, it was anything but dignified. But it was fast.

When I was about half a mile away from the Hoover Dam, I heard it. Barely. The white-noise roar of a wall of water headed towards me. The dam had eroded further. The water was coming. There wasn't much time.

I flew up a few hundred feet above the canyon, so I could get a good view. The canyon below the dam was not all good for what Licia had suggested. Some of it was deep and narrow, but in other spots the desert sloped steeply down, but not sheerly. I was trying to get ahead of what was coming to buy some time.

Out of the corner of my eye, I noticed that tour helicopter

again. It seemed to be following me. This didn't surprise me, but the green flash I saw jump out of it did.

Toxicwasteman.

Like Lightningirl and I, Toxicwasteman is a contained reaction, a chemical reaction. While my q-morph form is swirling motes of yellow, his is similar but a sickly green, iridescent green.

He was soon flying next to me, jets of green flame coming out of his feet, hands, and posterior, a trail of thick black smoke following him. He had developed his own chemical-based butt-thruster.

Now we both looked silly.

"This is going to be fun, Neutrino," he shouted at me. He sounded like some little kid about to get on a roller coaster and had a smile on his pulsing green face. "Let's do this!"

———

YOU MAY BE PUZZLED AS TO WHY I WAS SURPRISED TO SEE Toxicwasteman jumping out of the helicopter and coming to help me. You may have figured out who was in that helicopter the first time I mentioned it.

But I was surprised.

This surprise was part of what was going on for me. I tended to take people and situations at face value. Although it was an obvious thing, it didn't occur to me that LoVE would be monitoring this encounter or that Toxicwasteman himself would be on site just in case.

So I was surprised and mad. Mostly mad at myself for not seeing the obvious. For being so naïve.

"Next bend," I shouted, pushing down my anger and surprise, pointing to a narrow spot in the canyon. We were right in the middle of an emergency, this was not the time to get all introspective. "You take the right side, I'll take the left. Blast down low, let's see if we can bring down enough rock to slow the water down."

Toxicwasteman gave me his green-toothed wolfish grin in

answer. This was going to be fun for him, it was obvious. This was way too serious to be fun for me.

We dove down into the canyon, Toxicwasteman to my right and slightly behind me. We flew above the dark blue waters of the Colorado, tranquil and as yet unaffected by the coming torrent. And when we rounded the bend, we blew the hell out of the canyon.

I fired a rapid barrage of neutrino bolts low, just where the canyon rose sharply up. Toxicwasteman fired balls of green that exploded on contact on his side.

We were a mile or so down from the dam. We both circled around to survey the damage. Rock from both sides had fallen into the river forming a low dam that reached barely above the water level. It wasn't enough. Not nearly enough.

We hovered there staring.

"You are going to have to go elemental," Toxicwasteman said.

"No shit," I shot back. Yes, I was a bit grumpy. I don't like going elemental, and I certainly didn't like him pointing it out, but I didn't see a choice.

13 / ELEMENTAL

I HAD DONE IT WHEN I HAD TAKEN ON THE METEOR THE aliens had sent towards the Earth. Just like Licia has an elemental electrical form, when she travels on high-tension power lines and when she fought at the Battle of Palo Verde, I have one too. Except mine is kind of like turning into a nuclear bomb. I explode.

In that brief time that we paused above the Colorado River downstream from the badly damaged Hoover Dam, a wall of water fifty feet high came roaring down the canyon. I heard it first, like a massive wall of white noise, and still I was not prepared for the sight of it. The water was surging and sloshing down the canyon, a wall of it five stories high, a hungry torrent splashing up the sides of the canyon. It was epic.

I surged forward, flying low over the river as fast as I could. I flew so fast, I left Toxicwasteman behind, which gave me some sliver of satisfaction.

I wanted a spot where the canyon narrowed, before Lake Mohave started. There were only a few miles to go until the upper end of the lake and I feared I wouldn't find it.

And then I did. It was on a straight portion, but the canyon was narrow and the right side had already been undercut a bit by the river. I increased my reaction to the max, carefully containing most of my energy, and slammed into the cliff. I let my reaction bleed hot and I could tell the rock around me was melting as I burrowed farther into the canyon.

I explained this "exploding" before. I let my nuclear reaction build and build, but I contain it. And then, just like a balloon, it becomes too much and explodes forth. I explode.

And that is what I did.

I went elemental and for a few moments there was no Neutrinoman anymore.

———

I HONESTLY HATE GOING ELEMENTAL. IT'S KIND OF LIKE WHEN Quinn becomes The Hammer, he loses a lot of himself to become a more primal being. Going elemental, exploding, is like that times one hundred. The essential me is gone and I never know what's going to happen or where I'm going to end up.

And this time where I "ended up" was in total darkness unsure of where I was or what had happened. I felt a suffocating pressure all around. Where was I?

I was still Neutrinoman—which was fortunate or I wouldn't have survived. I instinctively ramped up my reaction and the earth started to glow and melt around me. I couldn't see much but the orange-yellow glow of molten rock, but at least I could see something.

So rock... I must be underground. It started to come back to me. Hoover Dam breached. Flood waters heading downstream. I could tell which way was up by how the rock flowed around me. I started thrusting upwards with my hands and feet making my way towards the surface.

It was taking a long time and I started to freak out a bit. One part "buried alive" and another part "did it work?" I started going faster and faster, tunneling my way up, melting through the rock and earth. I could feel my energy depleting. I hoped I had enough left in me to get out. And just as my mind was telling me I would die here alone burned to death by the rock I was melting, I burst forth through a massive pile of loose rock into a bright and beautiful desert morning.

The cliff that I had burrowed under was now slumped into the canyon forming a barrier four hundred feet tall. It had worked. Water was building behind it, some of it seeping through the bottom of the impromptu dam, but not much.

It worked.

I flew over, inspecting it, seeing if it looked like it would hold. It wasn't a tall, tapering dam like Hoover had been. It was a thick jumble of rock and dirt clogging the canyon. Not elegant, but serviceable.

I looked back and saw that the explosion had been directed. Earth didn't go everywhere, most of it went directly into the canyon. And that's the thing about being elemental. I'm gone, but not completely. My intent, to block the canyon, came through.

That's when I noticed Toxicwasteman standing on the opposite cliff. He was smiling and waving for me to come over, like we were both eight years old and his mother had just baked cookies. No, that's not right. He was waving like a twelve-year-old that had just found his older brother's secret stash of Playboy Magazines and wanted to show it off.

SPRING 2005, COLORADO RIVER, NEVADA/ARIZONA BORDER

"WELL DONE, NEUTRINO," TOXICWASTEMAN SAID AS I LANDED beside him. We had a good view of the river and the new dam. The water was sloshing behind it, a thick brown, the color of chocolate milk.

He extended his green hand for me to shake but I ignored him.

"Right," he said. "We don't have much time."

I didn't know what he was talking about, so I ignored that comment too. "Do you think it will hold?" I asked.

He nodded. "Over ninety percent chance," he said. "It will hold long enough for the dams downstream to prepare."

I looked away from the churning water and back at him. How the hell did he know that?

He saw the question on my face and turned his head and pointed at his left ear. In it I could see a little metal earbud—he was in communication with someone. I also noticed that the green swirls of his Toxicwasteman form were less pronounced around his ear. They had figured out a way to get comm equipment on him. I was jealous.

"We've been simulating everything live," he said. "Byte sends on her congratulations." He gave me an exaggerated wink, making me remember Byte's offer to me in her crystal cave in the LoVE base.

"So you know they're pissed, right?" Toxicwasteman said.

"What?"

"The military. They are *so* pissed. You let Chaosboy go. You oversaw the destruction of the Hoover Dam. And you didn't tell them a thing, not one tiny little thing about it." He held his green index finger and thumb close together. "It's that last bit that really has their panties in a bunch."

Well... when he put it that way. "Yeah, I guess they are. But I was—"

Toxicwasteman held his hand up, cutting me off, and tilted his head. Byte must have been talking to him. His expression fell as he slowly nodded his head, suddenly looking very serious.

"Okay, listen up," he said, turning back to me. "There's not much time at all now. I know you have some questions, so I'm going to just answer them." He didn't give me a chance to say anything and plowed right on. "One, there is a good chance that Gaia survived. Byte has reviewed the footage we shot and done her simulation thing and we believe she withdrew down into the Earth fast enough to not get injured."

I nodded, glad to hear that. I hadn't wanted to hurt her.

"We will do our best to send her back your way," he said.

"Send her my way?" I asked.

"You and Lightning were getting through to her," he said. "Surprising, really. But true."

His insistence on calling me Neutrino and Lightningirl Lightning was really starting to annoy me. The suffix of "man" or "girl" reinforced our humanity, which I have found important with the power we wield.

"Next, we believe that the military has been observing you this entire time. Is observing you right now, you apishly dense Boy

Scout! We've got to do some damage control!" He was yelling at me now, gesticulating wildly with his hands, which made absolutely no sense.

"What are you—" I began.

"No time!" he yelled. "Just listen. You aren't going to like what comes next. I am going to fly away and you are going to have to make a good show of trying to stop me. But, please, just make it a show."

"What?" I was still confused. I didn't know what he was talking about and why he kept yelling.

"Just fly after me and fire a few neutrino bolts, then turn back, look concerned about your little dam here, and then come back. They'll be here soon, you yellow excessively moral buffoon! And when they come, your best bet is to go in easy!"

Now I was just getting angry. A sickly green super villain yelling at you will do that. Not having the full picture—ever—will do that. Realizing that during your secret "off book" adventure everyone was watching your every step, will certainly do that.

Toxicwasteman turned, as if he was going to go, and then swung around fast, his green fist connecting with my yellow chin. Hard. I went down.

We established this in Yellowstone, Toxicwasteman and I don't mix. Where his green toxic touch connected with my chin, I felt a sharp, deep pain and knew that I had been infected with his greenness.

He laughed, a high-pitched manic kind of thing, flexing his fist which had a patch of yellow on it from our contact. It looked like it hurt him too. He then turned and flew away, trailing thick, black smoke.

He didn't have to remind me to fly after him. I wanted to. He didn't have to remind me to shoot neutrino bolts at him. I gladly did.

He flew low above the river and I followed. One bolt grazed his back and he glanced back at me, then. The look on his face is an image I'll treasure. He was scared. He thought I was really going to take him down.

I wanted to. But I didn't.

I fired a few more bolts, came to a halt, and gazed back at the dam I had created with a worried look on my face. I looked back at the retreating Toxicwasteman once more and then went back to monitor the dam.

Just as I had been instructed to do.

The truth was I didn't know enough to do anything else. Toxicwasteman hadn't given me enough information. No one ever gave me enough information.

As I landed back on the cliff and watched the muddy water build behind the thick rock dam, I heard the thump-thump of helicopters approaching. They were coming.

15 / STANDOFF

ONE HELICOPTER BUZZED AROUND ME BRIEFLY BEFORE leaving. I ignored it. I was firing neutrino bolts at the cliff just in front of me trying to force more rock into the canyon. I really was worried about the dam holding long enough.

In my training with the military, I have found that not all neutrino bolts are created equal. I can fire some that will go a long way and remain hot. I can fire others that are short range and will explode. I was working with the latter here, trying to modulate them so they didn't have much range, just enough to get a few feet into the rock, but had a great big bang.

It was working pretty well. I was slowly carving off more of the cliff, the side I hadn't exploded earlier. This is where Toxicwasteman and I had had our conversation.

I wanted to go check on Licia. I wanted to—and this is a surprise—have a long conversation with Toxicwasteman. I was doing my best, but I didn't have enough information. Licia might have some wise words on how to get more information out of him. And I knew Toxicwasteman knew a lot more than he had told me.

And then it occurred to me. In some ways both the military and Toxicwasteman treated me the same. They gave me just enough information to get me to do what they wanted me to do.

And that produced anger. And that next neutrino bolt I fired was a whopper. The sound of the explosion rumbled through my feet and the rock underneath me fell. I used my neutrino jets to hover while a full ten feet of the cliff slumped off and tumbled into the canyon, splashing into the frothing brown water, making the dam bigger.

It was then that I noticed the three dull-green UH-1 choppers. They were hovering around me, the open side door of each facing me. In each chopper was a soldier holding one of the alien energy weapons, the ones that could drain my power and return me to flesh and blood. They were all aimed at me.

And there is no mistaking these alien energy weapons with their bright metallic barrels and black tube snaking around to a big backpack. I hate them. I really do, and even though I was Neutrino-man, the sight of them made my stomach turn over.

"Stand down, Neutrinoman," a voice said over a loudspeaker on a fourth helicopter that was a ways off. "Find a place to land and return to your human form."

Now the military was threatening me. Great. Just great.

———

TOXICWASTEMAN HAD TOLD ME TO "GO IN EASY." I REALLY didn't want to but saw no other acceptable choice. I flew over on top of the cliff, landed, and let go of my neutrino form.

Those three helicopters kept hovering, soldiers pointing the alien energy weapons at me.

And I knew those weapons well. I had first encountered them at Yellowstone when aliens wielded them against me, and then a larger version at the Battle of Palo Verde. And I had encountered them repeatedly over the last few months in training with the military.

Soldiers shooting them at me had become part of my training. They wanted to find out if I could build up a tolerance, so they had shot me repeatedly with those purple balls of energy. It hurt like hell each and every time, and while I had begun to find ways to resist them, I wasn't very good at it. The threat was real.

The fourth helicopter landed twenty yards away. I just stood there naked, covering myself as best I could, and watching the brown water build up against the dam. The morning air was cool and dry, the heat of the day not yet here.

I've talked about my lack of a costume, that no material can survive my transformation to Neutrinoman. How it causes me constant embarrassment. It's my upbringing. Maybe if I was born in France or was psychotic like Toxicwasteman, I wouldn't care about letting it all hang loose. But I do.

When the two soldiers jogged over with their rifles pointed at me, I had my hands over my genitals and red blossoming on my face. I think part of it is the transition: going from being a contained nuclear reaction to being mere flesh and blood is kind of a letdown. And by "kind of" I mean, "oh my God, is it a massive letdown."

Being Neutrinoman can be addictive. And in that moment of vulnerability, naked, the desert morning light of Nevada reflecting on the disaster I was just a part of, with soldiers pointing guns at me... Well, it can be a long way to fall.

"Hands up," one of the soldiers said. He was young, maybe nineteen, and he looked scared.

"No," I said quietly. "Bring me something to wear and I'll be happy to put my hands up."

It was a line for me in that moment. Being naked in that situation was one thing, but at least I was able to cover myself. I just wasn't willing to let go of what little dignity I had left.

"Hands up now," the other soldier said. He was in his twenties and had a hard look on his face, like he'd seen battle, like he would fire upon me.

I smiled, as best I could, and shook my head. "Get me a jacket and I'll go in quietly." I left the "or else" unsaid. I figured these boys could think that through.

We had a bit of a standoff there. Three helicopters hovering around me with their now useless energy weapons pointed at me (they work against Neutrinoman, not flesh and blood). One helicopter on the ground twenty yards off, two more soldiers coming forth. Two nervous young men with automatic weapons pointed at me.

I don't know. Maybe it seems like a silly time and place to make a stand, especially such a small one. But it was an important moment. It may have been a small thing, but I wasn't willing to budge.

Give me dignity or give me...

Give me what? Young soldiers firing on me? A direct conflict with the military? Becoming a fugitive? Death?

I wasn't worried about death right then. I had enough juice left to turn into Neutrinoman and fast. The odds of them delivering a killing shot before that were not that great. The military had been training me. Constantly. For months. I had plenty of tricks up my sleeve.

And while I couldn't withstand those purple energy balls, I was pretty sure I could evade them and I knew I could outrun the helicopters.

And then I thought of Licia. What kind of position would that put her in? Had they arrested her too? The weight of what had just happened crashed down upon me. I had dragged her into this, my stand here could cost her even more. And what about my parents? What would happen to them if I didn't "go in easy."

With a sigh, I raised my hands in the air.

Before I knew it, the older soldier had me on the ground face-down and zip-tied my hands together. He wasn't gentle in the least. He pulled me up and marched me to the waiting helicopter.

I laughed. I was Neutrinoman, what the hell good did zip-ties do? I heard the sound of my own laughter as it bounced off the bare rock, rose above the sound of the roaring river. I sounded a bit manic. It sounded a bit like Toxicwasteman.

16 / AFTER THE DAM BREAKS

THE EASTERN PORTION OF THE HOOVER DAM WAS BADLY damaged. Where Gaia had been, where she had beat on the dam with her giant fists, there was a large gash about two hundred feet tall and one hundred feet wide at the top, narrowing as it went down, forming a ragged V.

A huge torrent of water was flowing through the gap down into the river gorge. The generating station wasn't even visible anymore under the onslaught of mud-colored water. The darker color was caused by all the silt at the bottom of the lake mixing in with the clean water at the top.

Dams are not forever. They collect silt from the day they go into operation. The silt will eventually render the dam useless, although Hoover was far from that point.

The image of the crippled dam made my chest hurt. This was something that I had been a part of, something I hadn't prevented. There would be blackouts as they found ways to compensate for the loss of this clean energy. It would be massively expensive to rebuild the dam—if they even did.

This was my fault.

I got a good view as the helicopter flew by and then headed to the east over into Arizona. We didn't go far. There were a few green tents setup on the desert not far from the road. The helicopter landed and I was escorted, still nude, into the largest tent.

Licia was there pacing, her arms wrapped around her chest, dressed in fatigues way too big for her. Quinn was there too, back to his normal dark-haired self, standing quietly in a corner. There were several other soldiers, some communications equipment, a table with maps spread out on it, and Colonel Williams.

When Licia looked up and saw me, my heart almost broke. Her cheeks were stained with tears and she looked so small, not like a goddess anymore, but like a normal girl. She ran to me, ignoring the protestations of my two guards, and hugged me tight. I was glad that she wasn't handcuffed.

"It's bad," she whispered in my ear.

"I love you," I whispered back. Maybe not the most useful thing to say, but at that moment, for me, it was the most important thing to say.

"I love you too," she whispered back.

Another soldier roughly pulled her off of me. Licia gave him a look that could melt solid steel and shook him off.

Colonel Williams had ignored us thus far, but finally turned around. He's not a tall man but has this coiled energy to him. He looked fit in his army fatigues with short salt-and-pepper hair and a sharp chin.

He looked angry when he turned, but his expression changed when he saw me there nude and filthy from being thrown to the ground, my hands behind my back.

"For Christ's sake," he said loudly. "Will someone get the man a blanket, at least!"

Before long I had a scratchy wool blanket hastily thrown over my shoulders. The three of us, Licia, Quinn, and I, were alone in the tent with Colonel Williams. He had dismissed the other soldiers. I was still handcuffed.

Williams looked tired, he kept rubbing at his face as if trying to wake himself up. He was pacing the small space in front of the three of us. We were standing together by the edge of the tent.

"Perhaps I should explain," I began. "I—"

Williams held up his hand, cutting me off, and resumed his pacing. "Don't bother explaining, Nichols. We're past that at this point."

Past that? What the hell were we past? Things had gone badly, but we had tried our best. We had managed to mitigate the level of the disaster. We were past explanations?

"We know what happened," he said, walking to the table with the maps and pulling out a folder of pictures underneath. He walked over and showed them to us. Several were Quinn as Sadie, Chaosboy, and the three of us on the top of the Golden Nugget. The pictures were taken from several angles. They had had a lot of people watching us. There were also some grainy pictures of Toxicwasteman and I talking on the cliff above the river.

He took that folder back and brought out another folder. It contained the research about Gaia that Tom Tyree and LoVE had left for us in the suite at the Golden Nugget. I had stashed it in the trunk of my car, which is where they must have gotten it from.

I felt my cheeks flush again. Not so much from embarrassment, but from anger. Toxicwasteman had often told me about the "short leash" the military had me on, but I had no idea just how short it was. If they had followed us to Vegas, had they been observing everything we had been doing whether on duty or off?

I think Licia was having the same thought as I was. She was blinking rapidly and wouldn't meet my eyes. Had they been spying on Licia and me during our private time?

"This is serious," Williams resumed. "We have you consorting with, and letting go, two members of a known terrorist organization. You received intel from them. You took instructions from them.

You didn't inform us of your actions." He sighed, rubbing his face again. "God, Nik. What were you thinking?"

I opened my mouth up to answer, but he held up his hand again. "Don't tell me," he said. "This is beyond me and I have done what I can."

My stomach twisted sharply. Williams was the man that made our time with the military bearable. If he was out, what did that mean for us?

"I have a deal to offer you," he continued, his green eyes softening somewhat. "It is all I could do." He resumed his pacing briefly and then returned and stood erect in front of us, his hands behind his back.

"The deal is this. Nichols, you are going to be 'detained' and you will be the only one being detained providing that Lopez and Rask cooperate."

I didn't like the word "detained." I would prefer being arrested, that implies lawyers and publicity. "Detained" sounded much more nefarious and a lot more quiet.

"Cooperate?" Quinn asked.

Williams gave him a sharp nod. "Have you mastered impersonating him?"

Quinn nodded.

"Let's see," Williams said.

The click-squish sound started and I watched as Quinn turned into me. He was soon standing there, four inches shorter, with my messy brown hair, pale white skin, and a kind of goofy grin on his face. He still had his own blue eyes instead of my brown, but otherwise he looked just like me.

Licia stiffened next to me. I had told her about this, but she hadn't seen it.

Williams looked closely at both of us, slowly nodding. "You'll need contacts, of course, but that will do. And the voice?"

Quinn-Nik shook his head and said, "Not yet. Voices are much harder." His voice wasn't as deep as Quinn's, but it certainly wasn't mine.

I think it has to do with all the complexities that go into making a voice sound like it does. The physiology of the vocal cords and the tongue, the shape of the throat, mouth, and sinus cavity. The speech patterns and idioms of the speaker.

With the body, he had a visual reference he could use to match another's appearance. With the voice, he didn't have any of that. It was much more trial and error.

Williams bit his lip. "We'll manage. So the deal is this. Nichols, you go in quietly. Lopez, you reenter the program and are seen from time to time with Rask as Nik. Rask, you will make it so the world thinks Nichols and Neutrinoman are still on the job, still protecting us from the alien threat."

Back when Tom Tyree had first told me about Quinn, he said the military wanted to see if he could emulate my abilities. It was an utter failure, and near disaster. Quinn almost killed himself. I am a contained nuclear reaction, after all, and while Quinn can handle a lot of radiation, his forms are all flesh and blood. But what he can do is "appear" to be Neutrinoman. No flying or anything, but he can do a reasonable facsimile of the yellow motes and swirls of my neutrino form.

The air in the tent was thick and still. It was midmorning and hot now. I could smell sweat and fear. Not just mine and Licia's and Quinn's, but Colonel Williams's too.

"No," Licia said. She didn't say it loudly or quietly. She just said it like she was saying no to desert at a restaurant.

"What?" Williams asked, surprised.

"I will not cooperate," she said, her arms crossed. "If you think we did something wrong here, then accuse us of a crime. Arrest us. Give us a trial. You will not hide Nik away and have me pretend you didn't."

Williams pursed his lips and nodded. "This is not my choice. This came from General Markus directly. He wanted to 'detain' all of you. I convinced him leaving you and Rask free would be better for everyone." Williams sighed, his normally erect posture falling. "I can tell you that there are contingencies in place. There will be no arrests today."

"It'll be okay," I said to Licia. I could imagine what those "contingencies" were. There were more soldiers with alien energy weapons tuned to take Lightningirl and me out. There were armed soldiers surrounding our tent. I could hear the soldiers walking outside, vehicles and helicopters approaching. The only way out would be to fight our way out. I knew I didn't have the stomach for that and Licia didn't either.

"But..." she began, a worried look on her face.

"I promise you that if they take this too far, I will take action." I said it to Licia, but I was saying it to Williams (and whomever else was listing) too. "Put on their little show for them. Can you do that?"

Licia nodded and I turned to Quinn who nodded too.

"I will go in quietly," I said to Williams. "But I do have one condition."

17 / LEAVING LOVE

SPRING 2005, ARIZONA, NEAR THE HOOVER DAM

MY ONE CONDITION WAS NOT A LAWYER OR TO PLEAD MY CASE and explain myself. It wasn't clothing to wear—I still only had the itchy wool blanket. It wasn't certain concessions during "detention" or anything like that. It was ten minutes alone with Licia and no handcuffs.

And at this point, I had no doubt that we were being listened to, but at least we were physically alone. I held her and she held me. We silently did our best to reassure each other.

"I don't like Quinn," she whispered after a time. "What he can do..." I was holding her and a shiver ran through her body.

"Quinn is a bit strange, but he's all right," I whispered back.

"But how will I know if it's really you?" she asked. "I mean, he looked *exactly* like you."

"His eyes are always the same blue when he changes. He sucks at voices and always has that weird accent of his."

"And if he puts on contacts and figures your voice out? I just..." She trailed off. We were standing in the middle of the tent, her body against mine, that blanket wrapped around both of us.

"This really bothers you, doesn't it?" I asked.

She nodded and looked up at me, her brown eyes wide with worry. Not just about Quinn convincing her he was me. But about the whole thing. Me going away. Her back in the program. An alien threat that could come back at any moment. At the time, I thought she was focused on Quinn as a way to avoid thinking about those other things, but she always had better instincts than I did.

"Okay," I said, leaning down so I could be eye to eye with her. "Then we have a word that I will say so you know it's me."

She nodded and smiled.

I thought for a moment and then leaned close and whispered in her ear. The smell of her and her closeness was rather distracting. When I leaned back up, she had a quizzical look on her face and then recognition dawned.

I had whispered "pot roast" to her. It was the meal my mother had served when her family had dinner with mine. The day we had met. That dinner was my mother's attempt to set me up with a "nice girl." And it had worked, a fact she would never stop bringing up. I had also noticed that Licia, being a vegetarian, didn't eat her pot roast, just pushed it around the plate. Noticing that, I believe, had done a lot to get her attention.

It was such a mundane word, but for us "pot roast" has meaning.

"We're going to be fine," I said, pulling her into my arms again.

"Promise?"

"I promise."

We had too much to say so we just didn't talk. I held her tight. I held her past the ten-minute mark and didn't let go until Williams and several soldiers with those bulky alien energy weapons came in and took me away.

I was escorted across the hot desert to a waiting Huey helicopter, its rotors spinning fast. As soon as we boarded, it took off and headed to the east.

Licia was out of the tent staring at the helicopter as it rose in the air. Her hand was above her eyes, shielding them from the sun. She blew me a kiss and I blew her one back. The door to the Huey was still open and I had a good view of her.

I watched her stand there in the desert, surrounded by soldiers, Quinn, back to his normal look, coming to stand next to her. I watched her until we passed over a plateau and she was gone.

Even before she was out of sight, I was missing her. But, for now, this was best. But how long would this last? Where were they taking me? When would I be with her again?

Colonel Williams was staring at me. I sank down into a seat next to him and shouted into his ear so he could hear me. "I'm holding you personally responsible for her safety."

His eyes widened briefly and then he nodded.

I didn't know what the future would bring, but I was dedicated to being back with Licia as soon as possible.

My thoughts weren't for alien threats or for civilization-ending disasters. Nor were they for the Goddess of Electricity, Lightningirl. My thoughts were for the flesh and blood Licia, the woman I loved.

I had to find a way back to her.

"That's it?" Licia asked, her eyebrows high. She put down the stack of papers she had been reading on the glass table of our flagstone patio at Casita de Soledad. "Seriously, Nik. You're stopping there?" She took a sip of iced tea, the ice cubes clinking together musically.

The hot sun was edging towards the horizon, the blue of the sky washed out from the heat of the day. My pale, radiation-loving skin was sucking in the UV as my muscles relaxed from building our new greenhouse.

This had become our ritual of late. I would write early, then join Licia at the greenhouse, and when the shadows started to get long, we would come out here and she would read and we would relax.

I smiled. While her tone was unexpected, I took it as a sign she was fully engaged in the story.

"You've got your brown puppy dog eyes on," she continued, her eyes stabbing down at the manuscript. "You're on the helicopter watching me fade into the distance being taken to God knows where, and you stop?"

"Puppy eyes?" I asked.

She nodded. As the greenhouse neared completion, I had taken to writing more, feeling drawn back into the past, feeling the need to get to and then get through the dark times right around the corner. "Let me rephrase," she began with a laugh. "'Adorable, cute, but *manly*, brown puppy dog eyes.'"

We had been over "cute" before, and while it still made me a bit uncomfortable, I let it be. "We're at the end of this story. Two important q-morphs have been introduced. Things are transitioning and this episode sets it up."

"But... But..." she said. "They're dragging you away. The Hoover Dam is destroyed, Gaia is believed to be on the loose... We have no idea how long it will take Sarah to 'speak' and what the outcome will be. I mean, things are getting crazy."

"The next episode will be along soon," I said with a shrug.

"But, don't you think you should treat your readers with more respect?" she asked. "Not play silly games with them."

I opened my mouth to speak, but then closed it. This ending was a cliffhanger, much more than what I had done before. I liked to think I was getting better at storytelling. And then I remembered something. "Do you remember that night we went out to that fancy restaurant in Flagstaff? This was shortly after you left the program."

She nodded, a quizzical smile on her face.

"We had been taking it slow, being a mess together, when you said you wanted to do this. You knew the owners, close family friends. They snuck us into their private room in that historic house that had been converted into a restaurant."

"Yeah," she said. "Not sure what this has to do with your ending here."

I smiled, looking her up and down. She was dressed in her usual shorts and tank top, but I was imagining what she was wearing that night. "Remember that little black dress you wore that night?"

She nodded.

"When I saw you in it, I could barely breathe. How it hugged your curves, how it amplified your considerable beauty. You also had your hair up, with makeup and earrings. You were stunning, absolutely stunning."

She was smiling now. "I remember."

"That dress, it was a promise that there was something wonderful coming." I paused, feeling my cheeks flush from the memory of that promise fulfilled. "You knew exactly what you were doing, I knew what you were doing too, and we both loved it."

Her brow furrowed. "Are you comparing the ending of this story to that evening, to... to..."

"No. No." I held my hands up. "Of course not. All I am saying is that dress was a promise, one we both knew we were making to each other. The ending of this story is a promise too. One that the readers know about and are used to. I am promising if they come back there is much more to come. I am promising the story of how our hero and heroine overcome challenge after challenge and reunite."

She slowly nodded. "But they'll want more right away."

"Yes. And just like the promise that black dress made, sometimes waiting, sometimes anticipation makes it that much better."

She reached across the glass patio table and grabbed my hand, a devious smile on her face. "You know, I still have that little black dress."

"Really?" I said. That dress is a legend in my mind, marking a turning point in our relationship.

"If you make us a nice dinner tonight," she said with a smile, "maybe I'll put it on."

We switch off on cooking duties and it was her turn. Also the word "nice" signaled that she wanted something more than baked potatoes, steamed veggies, and a bunch of cheese.

"What do you mean?" I asked. "It would take all of two minutes to put the dress on. Why do I have to make dinner?"

She smiled broadly and got up. She moved slowly and sensuously—quite on purpose, I am sure. "You can't just put on a dress like that," she said. "I need a bath first and time to primp. It's not just a dress, you know. It's the mood and attitude. That takes time."

I was nodding, watching her walk to the sliding glass doors that lead into our casita. "Besides, didn't you just say that sometimes anticipation makes these things better?"

I nodded and watched her go into the house and close the door behind her, full of anticipation of what was to come.

I sat there happy as could be, unaware of the change that was about to descend on our current lives. The seeds had been sown, but I didn't have a clue what was coming.

EPISODE 5

HARD TIEMS

THERE IS MORE ADVENTURE, MORE FUN, MORE *NEUTRINOMAN and Lightningirl* coming soon in episode 5, *Hard Times.* Sign up for my newsletter at RobertJMcCarter.com/newsletter and don't miss a thing.

And for the same kind of romantic adventurous fun as *Neutrinoman and Lightningirl* set in post-apocalypse Arizona, check out *Woody and June versus the Apocalypse.* Join the fan club at Woody-AndJune.com and get the first two episodes for free!

⸺

WOODY AND JUNE VERSUS THE APOCALYPSE

Love and the Apocalypse

When Woody Beckman meets June Medina, neither expects the adventures that will follow. Dedicated go-it-alone survivors, they've learned not to trust anyone in post-zombie-apocalypse Arizona.

But when regular-guy Woody must save tough-as-nails June, they realize that to survive they must learn to trust each other.

As the pair deals with everything from zombies to psychotic, petty, wannabe warlords to the harsh Arizona deserts, they start to realize that they might just prefer facing this crazy world together.

A story of adventure and love and taking things (even the apocalypse) in stride.

Get the first two episodes for free by joining the fan club or go grab Volume 1 with all 7 episodes!

ABOUT THE AUTHOR

Robert J. McCarter is the author of seven novels, three novellas, and dozens of short stories. He is a finalist for the *Writers of the Future* contest and his stories have appeared or are forthcoming in *The Saturday Evening Post, Pulphouse Fiction Magazine, Fiction River, Andromeda Spaceways Inflight Magazine,* and numerous anthologies.

His latest effort is a serialized novel called *Woody and June Versus the Apocalypse,* a story of adventure and love and taking things (even the apocalypse) in stride. Of his novel, *Seeing Forever,* Kirkus Reviews says, "Sci-fi as it should be: engaging, moving, and grand in scope."

He lives in the mountains of Arizona with his amazing wife and his ridiculously adorable dogs.

Find out more at:
robertjmccarter.com

BOOKS BY ROBERT J. MCCARTER

NEUTRINOMAN & LIGHTNINGIRL: A LOVE STORY

- Meteor Attack!
- Toxic Asset
- Protocol X
- Season 1 (Omnibus edition of Episodes 1 - 3)
- Off Book
- Hard Times (coming April, 2020)
- Elemental Factors (coming June, 2020)
- Season 2 (Omnibus edition of Episodes 4-6, coming August , 2020)

Find out the latest at Neutrinoman.com

WOODY AND JUNE VERSUS THE APOCALYPSE

1. Woody and June versus the Wannabe Warlord
2. Woody and June versus the Fungus-Head Zombies
3. Woody and June versus the Grand Canyon
4. Woody and June versus the Ex
5. Woody and June versus the Third Wheel
6. Woody and June versus Phantom Company
7. Woody and June versus the Daring Rescue
8. Volume 1: Episodes 1-7 (all seven episodes for a great price)

Join the Woody and June Fan Club at WoodyAndJune.com

NOVELS IN THE "GHOST'S MEMOIR" WORLD:

- Shuffled Off: A Ghost's Memoir, Book 1
- Drawing the Dead
- To Be a Fool: A Ghost's Memoir, Book 2
- Of Things Not Seen: A Ghost's Memoir, Book 3
- A Boy, a Girl, and a Ghost

OTHER NOVELS:

- Seeing Forever

For a complete list, go to RobertJMcCarter.com